AUNT LUTE BOOKS
San Francisco

THE LOWEST BLUE FLAME BEFORE NOTHING

by Lara Stapleton

First Edition
10 9 8 7 6 5 4 3 2 1

The publication of this work was in part made possible by grants from the National Endowment for the Arts and the California Arts Council.

Cover Art: "Bookdreams," copyright © 1995 Anna P. Oneglia.
Cover and Text Design: Kajun Design
Typesetting: Kajun Design

Senior Editor: Joan Pinkvoss
Managing Editor: Shay Brawn
Production Support: Livia Tenzer, Corey Cohen, Golda Sargento, Shahara Godfrey

This is a work of fiction. In no way does it intend to represent any real event or person, living or dead.

Aunt Lute Books
P. O. Box 410687
San Francisco, CA 94141

Library of Congress Cataloging-in-Publication Data
Stapleton, Lara.
    The lowest blue flame before nothing : short stories / by Lara Stapleton.
        p. cm.
        Contents: The lowest blue flame before nothing – Motherlove – No such absolute – The middle of October – Promise – Thirty seconds – Delicious –So much – The next place – Embouchure – The great artist – Pure impending glory.
        ISBN 7-879960-54-0 (alk. paper)
    1. United States—Social life and customs—20th century—Fiction.
    2. Philippines—Social life and customs—Fiction. 3. Women—United States—Fiction. 4. Women—Philippines—Fiction. I. Title.
    PS3569.T3349L6 1998
    813'.54—dc21   98-30108
                                                              CIP

MANY THANKS to my family, immediate (Ma, Pa, Jim, Sara and Annie) and extended, in both continents—including the Sotelos, Rita Senatore. Aunt Lute!!! Joan, Shay, Golda and the whole team—I can't say enough! The generosity of the Ludwig Vogelstein Foundation, the University of Michigan Hopwood awards, the New York University Writing Program and the *Columbia Journal* awards has been immeasurable! The editors of the anthology: *Flippin': Filipinos on America,* Eric Gamalinda and Luis Francia have been unduly kind! Thanks to all the magazines who have given their time over the years—listed on the following page. I must also recognize the champions: Nick Carbo, Bino Realuyo, Eileen Tabios and the rest of the astoundingly supportive family of the FLIPS list serve. The Nuyorican Poets' Cafe has been a site of inspiration and affection over the years. I think of two professors at Michigan: Bill Holinger and Tish O'Dowd Ezekiel.

And of course, thank God for: Aaron, Antonella and Bob, Arif, Charlotte, Claire, Denise and Jack, Deniz and Guinez, Drew D., Drew M., Garth, Gina, Heidi Holst-Leestma, Helen, Irene, Jamesnaman, Jeanne, Joel, Judy Moon, Julie Cadle, Justine, Maija, Mark and Veronica, Mark T., Mike Cheng, Noel J., Noel V., Paulo, Petra, Rachel and Daniyel, Ray, Rina la Reina, Robert and Nani, Rosanna and John, Saleh, Sherry, Su, and Veronica and Mark.

for Sara

The following stories were previously published:

"Embouchure" originally appeared in *Indiana Review*, Vol. 19, No. 2, Fall 1996.

"The Lowest Blue Flame Before Nothing" originally appeared in *Glimmer Train Stories*, Issue 19, Summer 1996.

"The Middle of October" originally appeared as "Fall Sourness" in *Nimrod: International Journal of Prose & Poetry*, Vol. 40, No. 1, Fall/Winter 1996.

"Delicious" originally appeared in *New Orleans Review*, Vol. 22, Nos. 3 & 4, Fall/Winter 1996.

"No Such Absolute" originally appeared in *The Antioch Review*, Vol. 54, No. 4, Fall 1996.

"Motherlove" originally appeared in *The Chatahoochee Review*, Vol. XV, No. 4, Summer 1995.

"Promise" originally appeared in *The Hawaii Review*, No. 46, 1996.

"So Much" originally appeared in *Another Chicago Magazine*, no. 28, 1994.

CONTENTS

THE LOWEST BLUE FLAME
BEFORE NOTHING

LOURDES AND LUZ would have a field day with the weight categories. Light-on-the-heavy-side-not-too-much-mayo-weight. Itsy-bitsy-teeny-weeny-weight. Fly-in-the-buttermilk-weight. Fly-in-the-face-of-convention-weight. Baton-weight. Bataan-weight. Needle-in-a-haystack-weight. Not-at-all-weight. Sneeze-weight. Lourdes, whose sophomore algebra was fresh in her memory, observed that light heavyweight must be like $x + -x$ and means you weigh zero, and that must be the lightest category of all. They went on into equations: what is junior dust-under-the-couch-weight minus wet-towel-weight? That's negative, clearly, Luz said. Okay, Lourdes said, Miss Know-it-all—toe-nail-clipping-weight by passing-wind. Disgusting, Luz said, and then they stopped, grinning. They bordered on ruining it by going on too long.

And later again, Lourdes would say that that was the turning point. Lourdes would say that that was the day which destroyed Dulce. They had lost her once and for all. Luz, who was the eldest and held greater strength of conviction, would say that it was just a coincidence, that that day, the day Dulce met Zuke the boxer, was only a normal teen-age act of rebellion. She would argue that she herself had done the same thing at thirteen, the night she drank three beers at Maria Luna Saguid's house. Testing limits, Luz said. You, Lourdes, she said—for a week straight you skipped ballet and made out with the Impala. Where did he get that damn Impala? I never made out with him, Lourdes said. We only drove around and held hands and they had money because his father had been a diplo-mat.

Lourdes begged to differ. Lourdes, who knew deep down inside that she was right but had trouble arguing with her elder sister, said that the day they met Zuke was a foreshadowing, a clear sign of things to come. And if they—the women, the two older and wiser sisters and their mother—if they had knocked some sense into Dulce back then, the later tragedy would have never arisen.

No, Luz said, the first time was normal—later it was crazy. Later, they had already lost her.

Beg-to-differ-weight. Shadow-on-a-cloudy-day.

Dulce—she woke that morning into a stillness all her own. Before she even opened her eyes there was a mint flavor, and her breathing stung slightly, a good cold sting, balm. From the moment she woke, she longed to be outside so her skin could drink the sun. She was euphoric. She was fifteen. She sat for a moment on the edge of the bed and blinked the sleep from her eyes. Lourdes lay in the twin bed across the room. Later, the three sisters would go to the international festival at the park.

For Lourdes, that day had been something else entirely. What she tasted was not something you're supposed to taste. Slightly poi-son. Like lingering paint on your hands, or soap. She knew from the start that it would simply be a day to endure. She couldn't lay her finger on it but it was everything. She *heard* the morning noises of the house—the pipes with their refusal of rhythm, her father uri-nating in the bathroom, the obscene swallow of the toilet. Her scalp itched. Her white bras were all dingy and full of lint. There was certainly a pea in the mattress, boy.

Lourdes tried to keep it to herself, noticing that Dulce was ecstatic, that Dulce carried the expression of a child about to break into run. Lourdes knew instinctively that Luz and Dulce would not tolerate her foul mood, would mock and further irritate her. And so she was silent. And so she didn't complain when Dulce turned the radio to a station that didn't come in clearly, when she let the static burn and sizzle through to ruin a beautiful song.

Dulce with her incomprehensible outburst of affection. She kissed her parents and sisters. She grabbed their hands and danced while the others were still staring with weariness.

Dulce pinched her shoulder blades back and put on her most womanly dress, a bright yellow thing that fell just over her knees. She looked curvier.

She was, indeed, the curvy one. Dulce was thick and brown, like her mother's side. Luz and Lourdes had the look of Chinese girls, like their father, slender and yellow. Dulce was the dark one. Her hair was just a bit coarse. For this reason she was their mother's baby, the island child.

Seemed Baning spent all her daughters' young years braiding Dulce's hair at the kitchen table. Braiding and unbraiding, braiding and unbraiding toward an absurd perfection. The other two were jealous and watched huddled from the bottom of the stairs.

That day Luz and Dulce couldn't stop touching each other, and Lourdes walked briskly ahead. The two linked arms. They pressed their cheeks together. Baning had given them two dollars a piece. They were to be home by nightfall.

Dulce imitated Lourdes' walk. She always walked like a dancer. Feet turned permanently out into second position. One arm squeezing a bulky bag against her side, one arm arranged with delicacy—that slightly extended pointer finger, that curve of the wrist. Luz whispered loudly enough to be overheard, "You'd think that maybe one day she would leave the house without her hair in a bun."

Dulce did her own big clunky imitation of a pirouette. Luz's was closer, being that she was slight-framed like a ballerina, being that her body worked that way. They asked if Lourdes would like to go back and get her tutu.

The sun was raging, interrogating, but there was a breeze strong enough to bring relief, goose pimples. The wind lifted Dulce's skirt slightly, and she liked it. Lourdes' skirt was a narrow fit, and Luz's defied gravity and stayed put. Dulce turned her face up and opened her mouth, as if there were a sweet rain. Lourdes looked for shade. She would walk swiftly ahead with her out-turned feet and then pause to wait under an awning for the other two. And then she'd do it again.

Their mother had packed them a bag and Lourdes had it squeezed under an elbow. Baning had insisted on giving them six large pork buns, each wrapped in aluminum foil. There would be food at the fair, but Baning insisted. She gave them a thermos of Kool-Aid. Lourdes could hear it sloshing as she stepped. They stopped in a little deli for candy. Lourdes' bag was bulky enough that when she turned, unconscious of her girth, things behind her got knocked off the shelves, and when she turned to eye the tumbling cans, boxes fell. Luz and Dulce snorted into their fists.

Lourdes reminded herself that sometimes you feel like this. That sometimes you have moods where little things mean more than they would on other days. Her headache was a barely perceptible hum, the lowest blue flame before nothing. She wanted to grab Luz by the hair, not Dulce, but Luz. Luz could so easily gather Dulce against Lourdes. It was Dulce and Lourdes who shared a room. Lourdes who spooned Dulce when she cried.

Lourdes was seventeen and Luz was one year older.

Lourdes grew increasingly resentful that she was burdened with the heavy bag while the other two skipped and fell over each other.

"You take it," she said, holding it at arm's length to Luz. Luz said no way, José, and then Lourdes looked to Dulce. She would have said please to Dulce, but Dulce looked to Luz.

Lourdes grumbled. There was the sloshing of the Kool-Aid and the embarrassing scent of the pork. She was a block ahead of the other two anyway when she paused to open the thermos. "Do you want any?" she asked with a seriousness that made the other two giggle. Luz shook her head with a choreographed stiffness. Lourdes poured the sugary purple slowly on the edge of the sidewalk as she walked. She tried to match the stream with the crack. When she was done, she threw the pork buns back at her sisters—the aluminum foil was hot by now, and they threw a couple back again and Lourdes didn't laugh but she sighed.

By the time they entered the park, the three were walking together. It was overwhelmingly crowded. Luz said it was a fire hazard. It was like registration, she told Lourdes, who would be registering for the first time that fall.

Lourdes wanted to go home immediately. It stunk in a gross human way. Dulce said they should go back and get the pork buns off the sidewalk and sell them for a dime a piece. Luz said it would be a nickel to lick the Kool-Aid off the cement. They bought lemonades and intricate clay dragons on sticks from a Chinese lady. Most of their money was gone. They ran into their mother's best friend's daughter and walked with her a while, until she took off with her boyfriend. A white girl wasn't looking and almost dropped ice cream on Dulce. Dulce cursed her with the dragon and then imitated her. They stood next to a bench waiting for a mother to take her children and leave. Dulce called them brats and waved her monster on a stick when the woman wasn't looking. The lady finally got up and the girls collapsed against each other and fanned pamphlets over their faces.

There were boys on fences. There were boys on fences all over the park, in pairs and threesomes and ten at a time. Lourdes and Luz weren't particularly fond of these young men, but Dulce, she couldn't help herself. Dulce had lingered a few steps behind whenever her sisters got distracted. Her spine curved up. She smiled back at the hissing calling boys and then ran with her secret naughtiness back in step with the other two.

There were two particular boys not far from where the sisters fell into each other on the bench. They were facing them from the other side of the fountain. The fountain blocked half of the tall skinny one but his friend was clearly in view. One was tall and skinny with glasses, clearly a sissy, and the other was short and also thin, but very muscular. The short one wore a T-shirt fit to burst and a loose pair of chinos. He had a lot of energy. He hopped up on the fence and then down, up on the fence and then down. He gesticulated to his friend and turned to watch girls pass this way and that. The tall one stayed on the fence. They were Mexicans. The short one had a buzz cut and thick undefined features, as if his face were melting. The tall one's bangs rolled over in front and were greasy.

It was obvious that the short one would do the talking. They were the kind of friends where the one would do the talking while the other stuffed his fists in his pockets, shrugged his shoulders, and hovered awkwardly. The tall one would stand back a bit, nod at what the other one said, and blush when the short one embarrassed him.

Dulce liked the short one. He had big, rich brown eyes, darker than his hair. His eyes were big enough that she could see them from her side of the fountain. She liked the way he made fists loosely at his side, how quickly he turned from one direction to another.

The short one said something that made three girls laugh. Three Mexican girls suddenly bent a bit and one with a ponytail looked back. The girls kept walking, and the short boy turned to his friend on the fence and raised his hands for a little victory pose.

Dulce kept watching until he glanced in her direction and then she looked quickly away.

He called across to her in Spanish. Dulce looked one way and then the other to make sure it was meant for her. "What?" she called back, scooching forward and upsetting the way her sisters were balanced against her. He called again and she yelled back that she didn't speak Spanish. Luz and Lourdes looked to each other. He called back in English and asked her her name. Luz yelled, "She doesn't speak English," and broke herself up, but Dulce yelled, "Dulce," and grinned.

The new friend turned for a moment to confer with the tall one. Everything that short one did was exaggerated. When he nodded it was meant to be seen for blocks, as when he shrugged or waved his hand in disagreement.

What the hell are you doing? Lourdes said through her teeth, but Dulce sat where she was scooched, waiting, and ignored her.

The tall one got off the fence and arranged himself against it. He leaned where he had been sitting with his elbows slung back and one foot crossed over the other. The short one gestured to Dulce, come here, come here, with big arcs of his hand, and Dulce stood and smoothed her skirt over her ass.

What the hell are you doing? Lourdes said again, but Dulce sashayed away.

Luz looked to Lourdes: "We shouldn't let her go by herself."

"We shouldn't let her go at all."

"So go grab her by the scruff of the neck."

"Go with her."

"You go talk to those hoodlums."

They watched for a moment as Dulce swayed back and forth like a four-year-old with her thumb in her mouth. Then they slowly went to join them. As they got closer it became apparent that something was very wrong with the short one's face. It was thickened and leathery and his nose was on crooked. His eyes were fine, but just the eyes, not the lids. The lids were as puffy as an old man's. It was like a doe behind a mask.

"I was just telling Dulce here," the boy told the older sisters, "I used to know some Filipinos and they was good people."

Luz and Lourdes stood close enough together and far enough away to speak under their breath without being heard by the others.

"And then you killed them?" Luz whispered but she nodded appreciatively in Zuke's direction.

"He ate them like the Jolly Green Giant." This was Lourdes.

"The jolly brown dwarf."

Zuke was indeed a very small person, smaller than Dulce, certainly, who stood out in the middle, giggling an octave higher than her sisters had ever heard, with her butt up in the air. Dulce with her thick calves, her solid limbs. The boy was just as short and downright skinny, but with these muscles tacked on. Each arm swelled out at the biceps, a snake with prey in its endless throat.

"My name is Zuke." He put his hand to the side of his mouth like he was calling across a canyon, mocking Lourdes and Luz for standing so far away. "This is my cousin, Rudy." He pointed to the tall one who rearranged himself against the fence.

Luz nodded with an enforced friendliness, as if hand were too far for grasping, like peace be with you from a few pews away. Lourdes smiled, but her top lip inched up in the middle. They didn't return his gesture. They didn't mention their names.

"Those are my sisters," Dulce said, this too with bubbles. "Lourdes and Luz." And Zuke said he never would have guessed, no, for real, that the two looked alike, but not Dulce.

There came a moment of silence. There came a moment of heat, no wind to break that unforgiving sun. Rudy pulled his shirt away from his arm pits and readjusted his glasses.

"Gee, it's hot," Dulce gushed, waving the bottom of her yellow dress around.

"Yeah," Zuke said. "I have to be careful, with the heat, you know. I have to be careful with my health, cuz I'm a athlete. I'm a boxer."

Dulce visibly gasped. She bounced up on her heels.

"Yeah, I'm a bantamweight. Rudy here, he's a junior welter-weight but he don't fight so that's okay. What are you?" he asked Dulce.

Dulce: I don't know *gush, gush, giggle giggle*

He: You look like... *[Looks her up and down. The sisters lean forward, mouths open in disbelief, then quickly sneer...]* maybe a featherweight. No offense but that's more than me.

She: *[Hands on hips, runs the scales in laughter]*

He: Or, maybe a junior. Let's see. *[Walks toward her with his arms spread, as if to grab her by the middle and lift]*

The sisters moved forward. The sisters, linked at the arm as one unit, took a step in, and Zuke must have seen it out of the corner of his eye, because he did not pick up Dulce by the middle. Dulce swayed this way and that.

Lourdes wanted to mash that mashed face. "We should go home," she called to Dulce, who ignored her.

"Look," Zuke said. "I'll teach you: heavyweight, cruiserweight, light heavyweight, super middleweight . . ." Dulce repeated and uncurled a finger for each category.

The breeze disappeared again. The sun made them moist, made them both squint and shade their eyes. Luz took a handkerchief from Lourdes' bag and mopped her brow. Lourdes fell to dreaming, awake, in the heat. In the dream she was dancing. There was a recital in which Lourdes had a cramp. It was the kind of thing, had it been in class, the instructor would have run to her with concern. Or the girl next to her would have known, would have grabbed Lourdes' calf and started kneading. Because they all know what it feels like when your muscles betray you. When that long thin muscle becomes a dense sphere, a filled rubber ball, an anvil.

But it was a recital. If you had looked closely, if you had known
what you were looking for, you could have seen it, one smooth
curving muscle and one sudden, relentless round fruit. Lourdes finished. She flexed her foot once but that was her only attempt at
relief, her only break. It was a minute or two. She completed the *pas
de béret*, the turn section, and the *grand jeté*. She finished on one
knee. And when it was over, she sobbed backstage and clutched
first her friend Angie and then Miss Ruth, as they rubbed the stubborn mass.

"How long was it like this?" Angie asked, and Lourdes said the
last half, and Angie said Lourdes was a heroine. They were still
clapping out front and it was Lourdes' glory, and Miss Ruth told not
only Lourdes' class, but all the classes except the littlest girls, who
might have been frightened, how very brave Lourdes had been.

Luz put her chin on Lourdes' shoulder and woke the younger
from her musings. Luz looked for Lourdes' eyes so they could stand
in judgment together. Zuke was shadowboxing. Zuke was a hero
too. He said *Ima buy a Lamborghini. Pow. Boom. Ima buy my mother a
fur coat. Pow. Pow. Whatchyou want Grandma? Whatchyouwant
Sinbad?* Aside: *That's my trainer.* Dulce fluttered. *Whatchyou want
Dulce?* He winked at her and paused, posing with his fists up. *Huh?
What you want? Chanel Number Five? Shoes?*

Luz and Lourdes had had enough and instinctively moved
together to take their sister lightly by the elbow. Dulce shook them
off. Zuke went on, he told Dulce how there was this fighter, he was
famous, you never heard of him? He's Puerto Rican. His wife had a
shoe collection and she would put sequins on them. That was what
she liked to do, glue those little sparkly things...

Rudy had been staring off somewhere else for a long time. He
seemed an ally to the older girls. The whole thing made him

uncomfortable. Luz and Lourdes each took an arm and tried to gently turn their sister. The grief stricken mother at the coffin, she didn't know her own mind and should be treated gently yet firmly. Dulce yanked her arms from their touchings.

The breeze came back, stronger yet, lifting Dulce's hair to black flames, her skirt. They all shivered. Zuke looked down at Dulce's legs. Lourdes bared her teeth. "Dulce it is time for us to go home right now." Dulce looked at her watch, said no, it's not, and made it clear that her sister was lying. Zuke started talking faster. He seemed to feel that if no one else could get a word in edgewise, they wouldn't be able to end the conversation. The girls stepped back and he stepped forward, reaching out and over with that babble— one time there was a fighter and that guy was already twenty-three and Zuke himself is only seventeen and he annihilated that old man how old are you Dulce... but he talked right over her answer. Let me guess. Oh I'm right—I figured. You could be older though, you got that sophisticated look, but I guessed... There was something panicked in his talking, and it gave both Luz and Lourdes the creeps.

Lourdes made Dulce turn to her. She didn't care if it was rude. "We are going home."

"No."

And then Zuke said, let me buy y'all some Italian ice. You girls want some Italian ice? And Lourdes said no, we're going home.

Dulce set her jaw. "Excuse me one second, Zuke," she said, with her shoulders up around her ears and her spine curlingcurling. She, Dulce, that little girl, grabbed her sisters by the elbows and pulled them aside.

"I am going to get Italian ice. I don't care what you do."

"No."

"How are you going to stop me?"

"I'll beat you right here, I swear to god." This was Lourdes.

"Go ahead."

"Dulce, are you crazy? Look at him." This was Lourdes again. Dulce looked over and beamed.

"He looks like an assassin," said Lourdes.

"He's ugly," Luz said.

Dulce's head was shaking something Lourdes had never seen before. She had never seen Dulce so stubborn. She would not admit the possibility of anything else.

"Beat me."

"Ma will beat you when you get home."

"What are you going to tell her? I had Italian ice? She's going to beat me for Italian ice?"

"I *will* tell her." This was still Lourdes, and even Luz was shocked by the proposal of tattling. They were way beyond the years of tattling.

"Do what you want. Go home and tell Ma, or beat me right here, *like you could*, but I am going to get Italian ice with Zuke. You can come if you want." She walked back to rejoin he who was now her date.

Lourdes' eyes darted all over Luz's face. Luz should have done something. Luz was the oldest. Dulce would have listened to Luz. "We have to go with her," Lourdes said. She was about to cry. Luz scrunched up her eyes with an accusation of insanity. Lourdes' desperation was more ridiculous than the whole ridiculous situation. Too much passion for this dumb day.

Luz thought of who might see her. She thought of a boy she liked from last year's biology and she thought of Jenny who was always looking for a good reason to say horrible things. Luz did not want to be seen with that ugly hoodlum. They argued, but it didn't matter: Dulce went for the ice.

"It's just over there," she called as she walked with Zuke and Rudy. It made Lourdes feel better that Rudy went too, and she could see the cart from where they stood.

Zuke didn't touch her. He turned back to wave at Dulce's sisters.

And it wasn't very long that Lourdes took her eyes off of Dulce. It was just long enough to threaten Luz with telling their mother and complain that Luz could have stopped the whole thing, and long enough for Luz to say Lourdes was a big baby and that everyone was acting crazy. It couldn't have been more than a moment but there was Rudy, the embarrassed messenger, talking without looking up, his black glasses sliding down his damp face. "Your sister said she'll be home before dark." And Dulce was nowhere in sight.

The breeze disappeared.

The seething sun.

Lourdes took the leadership as they searched, shading their eyes. This was the first time Luz didn't behave as the eldest; it had been stripped of her. Lourdes just walked where she would, knowing Luz would fall in beside her. Knowing Luz should have done right earlier, if she was going to do right. They combed the park. They chased a yellow dress, and it was a Filipino girl too, until the wrong gesture cleared things up. You would know from a distance your own sister's vocabulary of gesture. You would know her pacing. They saw Rudy again, shuffling with his fists in his pockets, and he promised to look too, to tell Dulce to wait by the fountain, but Lourdes didn't believe him. They spoke to a kid or two from the neighborhood, but no one had seen a sign of Dulce. Lourdes walked around front of a group to get a look at a short Mexican in chinos and a T-shirt. She walked around to look him full in the face and the guy's girlfriend asked her what she was doing. She kept moving. They split up and met back at the fountain, and then Luz said, look we have to go home. If she gets home before us we'll really be in for it.

Luz said we'll tell Ma she went off with Linda. This was their mom's best friend's daughter. And we'll call Linda and tell her what to say too. No way, José, Lourdes said. I am going to tell Ma the truth. I don't care what you say. Dulce can't act like this. She has to learn.

They walked home with their defiant jaws. Nervous and mad at each other. Lourdes' headache pulsed. She had to stop and close her eyes to cool it. They walked by the Chinese food place, where an *n* had fallen off so that the sign read "Chinatow." Luz nudged Lourdes to point it out and Lourdes said so what. Then Luz said, "light-on-the-heavy-side-not-too-much-mayo-weight, itsy-bitsy-teeny-weeny-weight." And Lourdes couldn't resist and said, "fly-in-the-buttermilk-weight, fly-in-the-face-of-convention." And then she laughed so hard she forgot her heated brain until they got very close to home and grew at first quiet and then argued again about what to tell their mother.

Lourdes with her *poise*. Her placing one foot, then the other, on the stoop, the stairs. The toe before the heel. The precision of her fingers on the banister, the doorknob, her nimble darting fingers. Everything always placed, never put. Lourdes looked very much like Luz, a version wound up taller with posture, but Lourdes' eyes were all her own. Nothing like the rest of her family, with their eyes open and receiving, their come-what-may eyes. Lourdes' eyes were always planning, narrowing, focused.

Luz knocked. Lourdes' stomach surged. They would all be in trouble but she would take responsibility. Lourdes' prepared herself. She stood up, up. Baning answered the door and smiled. The two came in, and Baning looked out in the hallway for the third. Before she could ask, Lourdes blurted out, "Ma, Dulce went to get Italian ice with a boy she just met and never came back."

Baning's expression twisted. This would have to be repeated.

Luz said, "Oh, Ma, she just went with Linda and Linda's boyfriend and a friend of his. They promised to be home before dark."

Lourdes felt she had been generous because she did not say that the boy was a mash-faced Mexican boxer. Now if she told, she would make two of them liars. It would be two against one, and Luz and Dulce would be ganged up against her for months. She would have to sleep in the room with Dulce, who would be not speaking to her. Dulce with her broad back turned, with silence to Lourdes' stories. Luz should be the wise one. Luz should know right and save Dulce. Lourdes looked to her sister, whose expression of defiance was only meant for her. Luz's face was so subtle Baning would never see. Luz would make Lourdes look crazy to save her own ass.

Baning sighed and said nothing. Luz went to the corner store to call Linda from a public phone and then waited on the stoop for Dulce as long as she could, until their mother called dinner. Lourdes clutched a pillow in her bedroom, plotting how to teach Dulce. None of her ideas would take hold. Usually, answers came to Lourdes and stayed. Usually, she would think for a moment and she would know. But on this day, she would decide and then a moment later forget what the decision had been. She was malfunctioning, dizzy. She had to save Dulce, but… Luz was bullying her, but… The phone. The truth.

It was dusk when they ate. It was almost dark. Usually, Lourdes ate so neatly. Usually, Lourdes was the one who cut small squares of her chicken, or only ate so many noodles, and turned the fork over, back up, place each small portion in her mouth and wipe with the napkin from her lap. She ate more than anybody and took her time doing so. But on this night she didn't eat. Lourdes basically stirred her food. And when the doorknob turned, Luz, thinking ahead, before Dulce even shut the door behind her, Luz, with her mouth full of noodles said, "Did you have a nice time with Linda and her boyfriend and that friend of his?" her stern, warning eyes. Baning said she was a bit late. Was she hungry? No, Dulce wasn't hungry and she swooned past them into her bedroom and swooned onto her bed so that she could stare at the ceiling and swoon.

There is a certain way that aunts raise their nieces and nephews. They love them for their missing sister, the dead, ill, or indifferent.

A double love. Love for a ghost and then some. With weariness and heartbreak and a desire to stave off the disaster they could not stave before. Lourdes, years later, she would raise Dulce's son with a bit of restrained madness. She would be afraid to touch him.

MOTHERLOVE

AMANDA is from a little gutted-out town in the Midwest where they once made things they no longer make. The houses are big and old and in disrepair. There is plenty of room for children to play. There is drinking and sorrow but there is plenty of room for children to play. There are driveways and yards, front and back.

Amanda Amanda with the soft red hair and bright blue eyes like you were looking straight through her head at a clear shining day.

Boys did skateboard tricks in Amanda's driveway. They scared her with mice by the tail. They talked louder when she entered the room, yelled out each other's shames. They brought drawings from art class and air-guitar songs. They blushed and stammered, phoned late and angered her mother. Pebbles rattled her window, coins. They asked her to dance. They braced themselves and approached her and felt a slow cold humiliation in their bowels. They tried to win her with sheer endurance, they waited for the others to leave. They stayed until she left the parties. They hung around doors she was known to exit.

She got banana splits for the price of a cone and Big Gulps from Seven-Eleven for free. The bus driver went off route and pulled right up to her door. He made runs after his shift had ended. Firemen waved from their truck. Her mother brought Amanda when she knew there would be bartering, flea markets, used cars.

At her peak, Amanda's own charm was an act of cruelty. They felt it. She felt it. She loved it. She loved the way her smile made them quiver, the soft ache in air around them. She loved their various faces, this one with the perfect smoothness between cheekbone and chin, that with the green and gold eyes. The big manly ones, the swaggering pirates and the slim, witty artsy-fartsy ones. Football and saxophone and even the druggies. She loved it, and so she peered back boldly into their wet and longing eyes and laughed in heaves and reveled in the sense of her own clean sweet prettiness. She was in a perpetual flush of flirtation. On the bus, in homeroom through P.E., through her after-school job. "Oh, you goofball" she said, shrugging and batting her eyes. So they came back and they came back, until that moment—his bracing and her final honesty. I don't want you *that* much, I only want you *so* much, and then the chill humiliation in his bowels. This was her cruelty. She maintained their affections for as long as she could.

Her girlfriends were very much like her but not quite the same. They were ladies in lawn chairs, queens on servants' shoulders. They sat on the edges of pools with their tall cool drinks and relished the languouring sun. They dipped their toes in the water.

Amanda loved to sing and there was glory when she did it. She starred in the high-school musicals. She gave the choir director chills. She could take a note up, hold it out, and then jiggle. She would drop down into tenor, man registers. In the dark, before that packed auditorium, she'd belt to split the night wide open.

Amanda felt large large large and swelling—petite porcelain Amanda with her slim and graceful waist. She sang and her arms reached up of their own volition. She threw her head back and purred like it was just too good to be true.

There was no choice but for her to leave. Amanda's mother shook until stones fell loose in her skull. Her science-lab partner cried. Her girlfriends wrenched and squeezed her wrists and promised to join her.

Amanda went to the city where a singer would go. She stayed with the kind and generous cousin of a friend. Amanda stood on the roof and watched the lights, overcome with a sense of her own potential. She said O *Sweet Jesus what did I do to deserve this blessed life?*

It was not just that the city is full of pretty girls and singers. This is not all that broke Amanda.

There was this: She came in late June and most of the restaurant jobs were already gone and she went to forty-three places before she found one. She counted. Around seventeen she felt they were turning her away because her weakness showed, her infinite swallowing need.

Finally, she got in at an old Italian place and she made lots of money because she worked fifty-five hours a week. She sent money home. Her mother was shocked and pleased that Amanda had money to spare.

It was all new to Amanda and she became quiet and she became very very tired. The other waitresses didn't care for her so much. She never added to their jokes. She felt there was film on her brain so that her jokes could not swim up to the surface. It was like pond scum or a fish tank long past time for cleaning. At four p.m., during the slow time, the other girls collected around a distant table without her.

Amanda was weakened and weary and when she was weary she began to shake and when she shook she dropped things and her boss asked her what her fucking problem was. She felt her very posture fray.

She went to an audition. She put on her sunglasses and a black leather mini and puffed her hair to as much width as it would occupy. She was number twelve. She was smart and got there early. She sat in a plastic chair while the late-comers had to stand. She closed her eyes and exhaled. The other girls had their nails done. She had forgotten to take care of her nails.

And then there was this number thirty-eight. Thirty-eight was a slight redhead, wrists as slim as the necks of wooden spoons. She stood across from where Amanda sat. Her eyes were big and blue and her mini-skirt was made of denim. She was very very pale. Her face was longer than Amanda's. Amanda thought it would be funny to put her hand out to the side and move like a mime in a mirror. Number thirty-eight might get it. This made Amanda laugh and then it made Amanda panic and she left.

Day after day, Amanda went home smelling like garlic and oil and her skin became layered in a scent that wouldn't wash out. She was sour with sweat.

She sent money home and worked and worked, and prayed to Sweet Jesus for her strength to come back.

She spent entire shifts thinking about how she shouldn't have fried calamari for lunch. Her eyes sunk. She had a greasy sheen. There came a heaviness to her demeanor. She worked in the outdoor café and the sun beat down on her head. The part in her hair burned scarlet.

She thought in loops: piña colada, shell steak, extra napkins, creamy italian, vinaigrette, six Bass ale, a spoon. No calamari for lunch. Money to Mama. Laundry tomorrow. Absolutely no calamari for lunch. Next month when she has *that* much money in the bank. Next time she'll get her nails done. Next week she'll buy the trade papers.

Her feet callused to a half-size larger. Her knees had a permanent throb. She went home at night and noticed that her joints were that much thicker than when she had woken. Her face lost its contours. It was as if holding up her features at the corners, her eyes, her mouth, were more than she could handle. She sagged. She took on, at certain moments, a demeanor of absolute despondency.

Amanda always had the front part of the long row of tables that made the outdoor café. It was the worst section and others easily bullied her into it. She had resigned herself to this. Edmund Roy sat in the very first seat. At the other end was the sun. He had an early lunch and sat and looked straight into the rising white heat so he could watch Amanda as she worked. He wore sunglasses so that she would not know. It would be quite some time before she considered a motivation to his pattern.

He ate mussels and tucked the white napkin in over his tie. Sometimes he'd drink a glass of wine. The sun glared right behind Amanda.

Her lipstick was always smudged. Smeared over the line on one side and missing on the other. Edmund wanted to take his thumb and gently blend.

The gap between what he wanted to say and what he actually said was astronomical. It was a horrible awful thing he went through. It was a complete feeling of panic. He choked. He balked. He said, "Excuse me…"

She walked from where she leaned against the building and said, "Yes?"

He said, "…"

And again said, "……"

He cleared his throat.

He said, "… Could I have some more water please?"

Amanda stood in the corner and sighed. Edmund watched how her ribs touched her shirt on the inhale. He ate very, very slowly and drank a lot of water. He'd leave an extra dollar on the tip.

Edmund gained weight in the months of Italian food and he could feel new flesh on his face, in his lap. He could feel where sweat pooled. The day he absolutely, positively was to tell Amanda she was lovely, he noticed that his shirt bunched out at the buttons. He put it off until he bought a new shirt but then, that day, his nose burned red and began to peel.

He thought of all sorts of reasons to hate himself. He had gained weight and his hair was thinning. He could put five fingers of one hand and two of another between his eyebrows and scalp. His smile was lopsided. He had hair in his ears. His job held absolutely no opportunity for advancement. He was no fun. He imposed himself on his few remaining friends, who only barely pretended to be glad to see him. His friends' smiles weakened. They had looks of distraction. He lost what sense of humor he had. His jokes had no timing. He set up stories wrong, forgot essential details, told the end too soon. He said things into the dead air and people around him stared back callously. People around him had a tendency to have other things to do.

He had no comeback for insults. He made mental lists of every stupid thing he ever said.

He had been unkind to his mother before she died.

He took on a demeanor of absolute despondency. His mouth hung open like some absurd fish.

But Amanda. With Amanda he would be a vessel of absolute goodness. He would rub her feet until she moaned, each toe between his fingers. He'd make her his sweet-potato soup. He'd put a trip to Europe on his credit card, if his credit were good, or he'd learn to budget and save. He would move them into a nice apartment, further out of the city, but better than anything she could possibly have on her own. He'd get behind her as an actress. He would cook the meals so she'd have time to rehearse. They'd have a Gatsby-style reception and study ballroom dance for the occasion.

He came to her in increments. He said, "I thought it was gonna rain today."

She said, "Yes. But I am glad that it did not."

He said, "Keeping busy?" That was good. In that way she could talk about her own life.

"Oh yes," she said. "Yes, I have been keeping quite busy."

On his way to work, he passed by the restaurant and often saw her setting up, standing the umbrellas on the tables or distributing peppers. Once, he saw her buy a white deodorant with a pink cap and a bright pink shampoo in a little corner store across the street. He went in afterwards, saw that it was Lady Speedstick and Strawberry Essence and bought the same for himself. He rubbed a touch of each in the crook of his arm and slept with his nose in the scent.

It was she who pushed it that much further. That was perfectly clear. She stopped giving him menus. She said, "The usual?" She said, "Mussels in a medium sauce with a side of spaghetti?"

She had gone out of her way to remember him, and that gave him the strength to ask her her name. He knew from the bosses, from the other girls calling her, but this would give him the right to use it. Amanda. A-man-da. Mandy.

He was moving forward, but one day a stroke of pure luck made him take an unprecedented leap.

On a cool cloudy day, when it might sprinkle but not really rain, Edmund stopped in an outdoor market. He wasn't wearing a suit but his khaki shorts and a clean white sweatshirt. He didn't need his sunglasses, so they sat at the top of the space where seven fingers would go. He looked good. He looked at pyramid-shaped candles and goldfish bowls—things he would never buy. He smelled the various incenses and the saleswoman was pretty surely checking him out. He ate a skewer of Thai chicken and drank a pink lemonade.

And there was Amanda, picking up earrings and holding them next to her ears. She held them in a pinch, between pointer finger and thumb, and with the other hand she held a mirror. One after the other she went, hoops and beads and tear-drop shapes. She stretched her pretty white throat. She turned from side to side. She wore a bun, and Edmund could see the soft, free little hairs sprouting at the base of her neck. They stood up as if from shock.

There was the rage and surge of his adrenaline. But this time, he had momentum. He felt he had the rhythm of a hurdler. He felt the limitless nature of his own potential. He felt he could beat his chest, stand straddle at the top of the hill with his fists on his hips.

He came up behind her, touched her lightly on the shoulder. "Would you like some earrings? I could buy you some earrings . . ." His breath was close to her skin and his breath was fresh that day.

And Amanda. She might not have turned around. She might not have looked over her shoulder to see who it was, but whatever the case, she dropped the brass leaf with the turquoise bead. She opened her fingers and let it fall with a bounce to the table. It knocked other earrings and made a mess, and then she cringed and hunched. She curled her back to an old-lady shape and went hustling off through the crowd.

Edmund's insides iced. He felt it in the seat of who he was, in the most shameful places. He stood for quite some time with his hand poised as if her shoulder were still there for the tapping.

Edmund sank into the lowest quarters of humiliation. For those first several weeks, it was all he could do to make himself chew. Had she looked back? Had Amanda turned enough to see his stupid grinning face? Or had she turned just enough to free herself of his hand? Did she glance back as she scurried away? Did she know his voice?

Aloud, to himself, Edmund repeated, "Would you like some earrings?" He would imitate his confident mood of that day. And then, "Could I have some water, please?" in his normal mood of those earlier weeks. He wanted to know if the two phrases sounded like the same person. He did this into a tape recorder and rewound and rewound and rewound. Each time he became convinced of an answer, he would do it once more to double check and again become doubtful.

He made suds in his bathtub with strawberry shampoo. He put Lady Speedstick on his palms so he could smell it at the office unobserved.

He couldn't sleep at night, so he fell asleep at his desk with his nose in his hand. The boss pulled him aside and spoke of his lack of performance.

He added a physical element to his suffering. He went for coffees and soups too fast and burned the inside of his mouth again and again until his taste buds were shot. His nights were spent in ulcerous cankerous pain and his days were spent in stupor. His eating diminished to nothing. He would forget meals until he had pounding headaches and he was forced to figure it out. In six short weeks, he went from pudgy to slim.

He walked in front of cars. Bleeps and curses summoned him back to earth. He was lucky and only received bruises from a bike and two flung-open doors. He would suddenly and inexplicably, with all the power of his jaws, bite the inside of his cheek. He would give a little yelp. Sometimes, at his desk, with his head propped up on his Lady-Speedstick hand, hovering near the borders of consciousness, he would find himself drooling. There would be a bubble on his lip and a little puddle on the papers beneath him.

He said *Would you like some earrings…? Could I have some water…?* He said it in elevators, on the subway, in line in the grocery store. People sneered at him and some, mostly in groups, openly snickered. His friends disappeared altogether. It would be safe to say he loathed himself. It would be safe to say he was not alone in his loathing.

And Amanda, who had been throbbingly tired and busy, for whom it was a trick to get to the movies or get her laundry done, discovered the extent of her loneliness. She had her first day off in twenty-three days and lay in bed, staring at the ceiling, immobile with the weight of possibility. Her sheets and pillows smelled of garlic and oil. Her hair smelled of garlic and oil. Her limbs felt soggy and useless, like wet lollipop sticks that could not support her heavy head or torso. She thought of her boss leaning over to yell in the kitchen. He was very tall, and he would have to lean over to get close to her face. His eyes were open, fury-wide, and he said, "Are you a fucking moron or what?"

This made Amanda cry. She lay in her bed and had a good cry over her boss for a moment. She heard her roommate bustle about. Amanda's roommate had to have heard. But the kind and generous cousin of Amanda's friend from back home did not ask Amanda why. Amanda lay still for a very long time. And then Amanda became disgusted, and she summoned all her strength and showered and decided to get a haircut.

She realized her loneliness when the stylist went to wash her hair. The woman laid her fingers on Amanda's scalp, and Amanda, who had not been touched so closely since she left her mother, moaned. Amanda's eyes fell shut and her voice registered the pleasure. It was a soft moan that the stylist may not have heard, but Amanda knew and was embarrassed. It was all Amanda could do to keep her eyes from fluttering during the entire shampoo process. It was all Amanda could do to keep from burying herself into every soft part of the stylist.

When she got back to work, Amanda noticed, in passing, that the man who sat in the front was gone. She did not miss him in any profound way, but in passing, she noted that Mussels in a Medium Sauce had not come around for a while.

Edmund stayed away for seven weeks. One Friday afternoon, in the fall, he woke up naked on his bathroom floor several hours after he was supposed to be at work. He had been bawling, and not asleep. This was the state from which he woke, a stupor. It was then that he felt he had hit bottom, and there was a freedom in this. Then he slept, really and truly slept, the entire day. And the next, during his shower, he discovered that a moment passed in which he did not think of Amanda at all. He got to work on Monday and apologized profusely and promised things would change. He almost believed it. He felt a tiny bit better, and one of his co-workers, a woman, commented that he had lost weight, and she said he looked good, and Edmund felt better again.

In his late night musings, he decided he had faced the beast. There was nowhere to go but up and it could do no harm to visit Amanda. He trimmed his mustache and looked at his profile in the mirror. He practiced "Could I have some water, please?" in a whole new voice.

Edmund left work for an early lunch at the restaurant. On the way, he was seized by an attack of terror. He had just crossed the street and was standing on the corner and suddenly felt his skeleton contract away from his skin, collapse in a heap inside. He felt he might lose control of his bladder. He stood like that, shaking, for a good long moment. And then, he breathed, and he reminded himself that he had faced the beast, and that if he were to urinate like an infant right there on the corner, he would, in fact, survive. This thought gave him the strength to continue.

His old front table was empty. All the tables were empty and he sat right down.

It was mid-September and it was getting too cold for an outdoor café. The bosses had not yet decided who they were going to keep and put on the regular inside staff. Amanda's income had decreased dramatically, to insurvivable levels, though she was working more and more. She wished she hadn't sent so much money to her mother, that she had saved it for herself. She now wore a heavy sweater over her black and white uniform and stood with her arms crossed, leaning against a parking meter. She always seemed to be staring at the same patch of traffic. She leaned to guard herself against the wind, which was on the strong side that day. Two other girls sat smoking and doing crossword puzzles at a middle table.

Edmund's chair made a scrape against the cement but Amanda did not hear. He sat for a time waiting for her to notice. He cleared his throat. He kept his hands folded on the table. The breeze lifted hairs at the top of his head. He said, "Excuse me…," but it was one of the other waitresses who noticed first and yelled, "Yo, Amanda," and gestured with her head toward Edmund. That waitress did not look up at Amanda and she did not take the quickly burning cigarette out of her mouth.

Miracle of miracles, Amanda smiled. A slow sweet grin of recognition. Edmund felt his own smile open a split second behind.

"Long time no see," Amanda said bashfully, and her voice was high but hoarse, as if it were the first time she had spoken that morning. Edmund nodded and cleared his throat.

"Coffee today?" Amanda asked.

Edmund nodded and Amanda scurried off. She came back with the cup in two hands as if there were a trick to its balancing. She put it down.

"Mussels in a medium sauce?"

Edmund nodded. Amanda made a note on her check, put the check in her apron, and delivered it to the kitchen. She returned with a salad with creamy italian dressing. He had not reminded her of his preference. Her memory made Edmund beam. She went to lean again against the parking meter and Edmund ate and beamed.

When she came to collect the plate he asked for bread, and

when she brought the bread he said, "So how have you been?"

"Oh," Amanda sighed, a bit caught off guard, and it seemed to him for a moment that she was going to tell him why she sighed. It seemed she searched his eyes for a good reason to tell him why she sighed, but then she just said, "Fine. I guess that I have been fine." This touched Edmund immensely.

She stood, for a moment, silent, where perhaps there should have been more conversation, and then she went back to her parking meter. The sun had come up a bit so it wasn't as cold. She stared at that space in traffic. She put her chin on the top of the meter. More customers came and the young woman who had called, "Yo, Amanda," got up to take them. Amanda turned to look as the people sat down. It was a group of four.

Edmund's mussels did not come and Edmund's mussels didn't come. He thought he remembered the amount of time it took for them to cook, and before he even first looked at his watch, it seemed it had been that amount of time. Then he gave it another seventeen minutes. Amanda still stood with her chin on the parking meter. She'd stretch for a moment and then bend to the same position. Edmund watched the second hand go round and said to himself, "Two minutes before I ask…one…thirty seconds."

Finally, Edmund, with as much politeness as he could muster, said "Excuse me…," and just as Amanda approached his table, the other waitress, who had three salads on one arm and the mussels on the other, nudged Amanda, handed her Edmund's food, and unabashedly sneered.

Amanda said she was sorry sorry sorry. She blushed and rushed for parmesan cheese. She turned the grater over his plate. Edmund ate his mussels. He wiped his face a lot and tried to be quiet with the shells. He maintained his breathing. He did affirmations. He said *Yes I will Yes I will Yes I will.*

Amanda came to refill his water glass. The ice clinked as it rose to the top. She stood looking down as he chewed. She narrowed her eyes at him. She asked faintly, "Did you lose weight, maybe?"

"Will you go out?" Edmund asked. A morsel of food flew out along with some saliva.

"Excuse me?"

Edmund took a moment to swallow. He mopped his forehead. "I was wondering if that you might perhaps be willing to go out with me sometime?"

Amanda stood still and did not answer. Edmund became aware of his bladder. "My name is Edmund," he said. "And you're Amanda."

Amanda shifted her weight from one hip to the other and back. When she answered, it was more lack of no than yes. "Okay," she said and looked off into that patch of traffic. She shivered. She wanted to ball up somewhere warm.

Because Amanda had no days off, they arranged a day in which she only worked the lunch shift. They met at a Japanese restaurant. Edmund had been waiting and stood up when she came in. He had a cloth napkin tucked in over his tie.

Amanda's vision was blurry with weariness. She kept squinting to bring things into focus. Edmund looked cramped and horrified. His head turtled in toward his shoulders. They didn't talk much. Edmund asked her what she wanted and ordered for her. He asked her where she was from and complimented her dress. Amanda tried to think up questions to ask but she was too tired. When the waiter came back, Amanda absent-mindedly reached out for the drinks and there was a moment in which they both pulled on the tray and it very nearly spilled.

Edmund sat waiting with his fork in one fist and his knife in the other. He said would she like to go hang gliding someday? Did she like to dance, and if so, in what way? She told him she had been in "Oklahoma" and "Grease."

Amanda ordered two kinds of sushi and then just stirred them around on the plate. Her joints felt puffy, nebulous. Edmund had shrimp tempura and ate without looking up.

Amanda thought it would be horrible to kiss him. His mustache was long and shaggy with crumbs. His lower lip was frozen in a grimace. He was sweating too much and the long hairs he had combed down over his forehead were sticking at ridiculous angles. After they finished, he asked if he could take her dancing and she said she was tired and would like to go home. He said he'd see her there in a cab.

Amanda leaned against the door away from him, dreading that he might try to kiss her. There would be a horrible fish taste. Edmund's entire neck disappeared. His face looked like Humpty Dumpty on the wall without legs, as if someone pushed him down from the top of his head, down down into the car seat, down toward the whizzing pavement.

They pulled up in front of her building and she could no longer stand to anticipate the horror so she leaned in to get it over with. It was awful, but after the initial wave of nausea, Edmund put his hands to her hair. He touched her on the scalp where the skin was burned and tender. He touched her very lightly, and Amanda found that if she concentrated on his fingers and not the kiss, she could make her edges disappear. She found she could escape the kiss entirely and dissolve. Edmund touched her scalp and then he put one hand on her calf where the muscle was cramped. He kneaded the cramp into softness. They sat there until the cab driver said excuse me and were they going to get out?

Edmund followed Amanda up the six flights. She had to stop and rest in the middle. He kissed her there again. They got upstairs and he made love to her in tiny bashful increments. He felt he was a teenager who did not know when she'd say stop. Amanda hated the kiss, but she could numb herself to that. Any part of her he touched uncramped and then floated. She had had no idea how sensitive her nerves had become. When they actually finally had sex she didn't mind it so much, and she did like the way he held her hands.

The next day at work, management handed out beepers. They received a speech in the kitchen from the tall boss. The six waitresses and the three waiters stood with their arms crossed, their jaws muscled in defiance, shaking their heads and cutting their eyes. Except for Amanda, who only stared down in disbelief at the little electronic nuisance. She turned the thing over and over in her hands.

The boss explained that food had been left too long in the kitchen. That while they were out enjoying their cigarettes, or gabbing in the john, or flirting with some fat loser—Amanda took that personally—food was dying in the window. And so, he said, we will beep you. Me, or Nick the cook, we will push this button—and here the tall manager turned on a machine that looked like a heart monitor. There were a dozen buttons on the thing and the boss touched number seven, which was, of course, Amanda, and the thing vibrated in her hands.

Amanda experienced the sensation of pulling out of a town she knew well, watching it grow smaller and farther away.

They tested the machine many times that morning before the restaurant opened. Nick the cook, especially, had an affinity for the thing. They would be going about their routine, propping up umbrellas or wiping off last night's crumbs, and then zzzzzzz, the vibrations, which were, in fact, quite strong, and they'd all rush into the kitchen to see Nick grinning and saying, just checking. The machine could beep them all simultaneously or one at a time. Amanda was easy prey, and just before eleven he called her in twice to say you'd better be ready to do that when the time comes.

The whole afternoon, she got beeped every time she had a table and sometimes when she didn't.

"You gonna take this before it gets cold?" Nick snapped, pointing at a veal parmesan with his spatula. She was sure she had just checked the minute before. She would have sworn it had only been that long.

Once, he called her in just to say, "Stay on your toes."

Amanda was so completely harassed that she inspired looks of sympathy in the other two café waitresses who usually only seemed to hate her. It surprised Amanda how electric the thing was. It made her think of shock therapy or the things paramedics use after heart attacks.

When the lunch shift was over, Amanda had a short break before starting again for dinner. By this time, she was so frazzled and tense that her shoulders pinched up around her ears.

At the bar, she changed six dollars into quarters so that she could call her mother. Amanda had been thinking of calling her mother and could wait no longer. She checked her lipstick in the clean sheen of the metal as the phone rang. Her lipstick was all over the place and Amanda tried to wipe it off with the back of her hand.

"Hey, Ma?"

"Oh Amanda," Amanda's mother said, and her voice was sad and Amanda knew why because she had talked to her mother a few days before. Amanda's mother sounded choked up, and this inspired in Amanda such a rush of affection that her knees nearly gave way.

"Are they gonna do it?"

Amanda's mother made a little noise that sounded like a nod. Amanda's beeper went off but Amanda was on break so she felt the right to turn it off. Amanda's eyes grew wet. She could see her own damp lashes reflected in the phone.

"I'm gonna come home, Ma," Amanda said.

Amanda's mother said, no you don't have to do that. And then

Amanda's mother said, O honey O honey thank you.

When Amanda hung up she did it very softly. She stood for a moment with her finger in the change slot. She felt like crying and then, right away, felt like not a thing could make her cry.

Amanda went into the kitchen to see what Nick wanted.

"Where did you go?" He bit his lower lip and stared.

Amanda shrugged. She undid her apron and held it in her hand.

"I asked, where did you go?"

"I'm not on right now. I'm on break."

"Oh."

"Can I have my spaghetti for lunch now, please?"

Nick grumbled and gave her some spaghetti and waved her out of the kitchen with his spatula.

Amanda went to sit in the corner where the employees sat for lunch. She sat by herself. A group of four waitresses and one waiter had stuffed themselves in a booth not too far from her. Their smoke lifted and curled above. Amanda ate slowly, noodle by noodle. One of the girls was a blonde named Roz and she was telling the others about a date. She would shake her hands like she was cooling herself and everyone would laugh. Once, she stood up as much as the booth would allow. She acted as if she had tripped over someone else's ankle or a rug had been yanked out from under her. When she was done with the date story, Roz twisted her fork back into her spaghetti and one of the other girls said, "Can you believe this shit?" She held up her beeper. She whispered, but it carried.

"It's like a cattle prod," Amanda called over. A noodle was sticking half way out of her mouth and she sucked it up.

Roz paused, smiling, with her nose buried right into her pasta, and two of the others snickered. Amanda wiped some marinara from her chin. The conversation went from an impending renovation to who was working the banquet room and back to the beepers again.

Then, their break was over and the tall manager told them about the specials and explained the beepers to those who had just come.

Amanda had a very good evening. It warmed up a bit and was busier than it had been in a month. She seemed to have finally caught on to the rhythm of the place. She knew just when to lean forward because someone was behind her at the cappuccino machine and she walked into the kitchen when her food was coming up. She was able to do more things at once. She could grab a lemon and spoon and tea bag in one sweep, while the other hand searched through the dessert refrigerator. Someone almost bumped into her when she had two mixed drinks and a soda on her tray, and she simply swung the tray in an arc to safety and kept on walking. She could see that men were checking her out.

Nick beeped and she went into the kitchen and he asked her why she hadn't taken the spirelli yet and he asked her what her fucking problem was. The tall manager was there and his eyes blazed. Amanda explained that she had had a few frozen drinks at the bar, and that took extra time, and that she was on her way already when they beeped. She walked out shaking her head with the spirelli balanced on her forearm, and the same waitress who had said it earlier whispered, "Can you believe this shit?" as she passed.

Amanda showed the beeper to a table full of college students and one of the young men made a crack about where he would put it and then screw up on purpose. "Now, now," Amanda said, waving her finger and grinning. The young man asked her her name and where she was from.

Amanda asked one of the other girls if she thought he was cute.

And then Amanda remembered Edmund. She had made a date with him for the next night, her next half day of working. She would have to tell him of her plans. This made her a bit queasy, but she calmed herself by putting this information in a list of things to do.

She would have to pack, give notice, tell her roommate, tell Edmund, buy the ticket, find a subletter, buy some souvenirs—all of this as soon as she had the money for the flight.

Edmund spent the whole day wrapped in his exquisite memory. He relived every minute moment. He took his time, and if he could not recall something in exact detail, he would wait and concentrate until it all came rushing back. At one point he could not remember the order of two events. This was rather frustrating. This caused Edmund to turn his head to the side and tap his pencil on his desk and think intensely. He could not remember if he had first unlaced and removed Amanda's shoes, or if he had first turned off the light. He remembered that her feet were very deformed, blistered on the top any place where a bone curved up a bit, and heavily callused underneath, like she had never worn shoes that fit. He remembered that when this happened, his mouth fell open with compassion. He remembered that she asked him to turn out the light as soon as she sat on the bed, but he could not remember if he had got up to do it just then, or if he had first removed her shoes. He pictured her feet both in the full light and then in the dim illumination that squeaked in under her door. He could see it in both ways.

Edmund was stuck in this for a while. Edmund recalled this and recalled this, until sitting at his desk in the office at two o'clock in the afternoon, he actually reached out his hand to feel the slight weight, the slim and mangled shape of Amanda's foot. It was then that he realized he had held her foot, gotten up to turn off the light, and gone back to holding it again.

He was then able to continue in his systematic recounting until he came to where he had pushed the cab door shut and Amanda turned to speak to the driver as it pulled away. She had looked sideways for a moment to wave good-bye and then she turned to face fully forward and Edmund could see her lips moving quietly with the directions. She had the ten dollars in her fist. He had insisted on giving her this for the fare. Edmund went to work in the same clothes he had worn the day before.

After he had savored every moment, in order, a few times, Edmund took to longing. He started imagining what he would do next. He pictured her in a pretty floral dress for a Broadway play. He pictured her on the beach. He would help pick out the bikini and pack the cooler.

He knew that he had been very, very gentle in his lovemaking. He was proud of having treated this girl with such tender hands. But next time, he decided, he would be passionate. This would be even more romantic. He knew just where he would take her for dinner next. An Italian place where they had little goldfish in ponds and fountains running. Then Edmund made some notes as to readjusting his budget. No more ordering pay-per-view or eating alone in restaurants. He would be going out a lot.

Edmund's boss called him into the office and said this was absolutely the last warning. Edmund smiled and nodded and assured him of change. Edmund chuckled to himself over the boss's pathetic life, his ridiculous sense of priority.

By six o'clock, Edmund was in a thorough state of desire. He decided it would be okay to stop by Amanda's job and bring her some flowers. It took all his restraint to go home and shower first, and then, as more show of discipline, he cooked and ate dinner, then browsed through two magazines.

Roz grabbed Amanda by the wrist in the stairwell by the bathrooms. She put a finger to her lips and revealed a piece of mud pie and two forks, which she clutched to her belly. They raced giggling up the stairs and stood in the middle stall shoving forkfuls into their mouths. The forkfuls were as big and fast as they could manage, and they both got chocolate all over their mouths. Someone came in and used a stall next to them and flushed the toilet, and they thought they would burst with their smothered laughter. They made all sorts of snorts and grunts. Amanda felt like she could drown with the laughter and the food up her nose. It was absolutely wonderfully ridiculous.

Roz got beeped and held the thing in her palm and gave it the finger. They wiped each other's faces and hurried out chewing.

Amanda still had some in her mouth when she got to her section. She approached her table of college students and had to swallow before she could speak. She rolled her eyes up and shrugged at her own naughtiness. The young man who had asked her her name then said that she was cute. When they left, he handed her his number on a napkin.

Amanda held the napkin in her hand and stood leaning over her parking meter. She let the breeze curl through her hair.

And there was Edmund, standing at the corner with a bouquet of roses in his hand. He waved in huge sweeps and walked toward her. Amanda looked over her shoulder to see where Roz was and then waved meekly back.

Edmund had on his face a look of complete and utter euphoria, a chilling euphoria. It was as if he walked toward her puckering from a block away. Amanda felt the chocolate hit her. She felt a nauseating sweetness stuck all through her teeth.

In a moment, during Edmund's quick approach, she imagined different ways of telling. *I have to go home it's my mother. I'm sorry it just won't work out. I made a mistake I just cannot.* And by the time he got to her, she had considered leaving in the morning, forgetting everything and not saying good-bye. His happiness was as large and oppressive as the severest of summer heat. She felt she would gut him. She felt he would collapse in a heap.

He kissed her and took both her hands in his. He seemed to suck her in when he inhaled. He seemed to reach madly for fistfuls. Amanda looked for Roz over her shoulder and she was not there.

He gave Amanda the flowers. He gazed sweetly into her eyes. He asked if he could see her home in a cab. "But I have two hours left," she said. He said that that was okay. He would wait. He stood for a moment and closed his eyes with joy.

Edmund sat down in his usual spot and ordered a beer and Amanda put the roses in the bus stand and went on about her evening. She tried to forget he was there, and every time she passed Rosalyn or one of the other girls, she b'zzzzed and pretended she'd been poked in the ass with a cattle prod.

Edmund saw the change of demeanor in Amanda. He saw that she threw her head back and looked people in the eye. He saw her elbow the other waitresses and chuckle. Every bit of her had been gathered then smoothed. He saw that he was right for her, that he was very, very good.

Amanda kept busy. She didn't have time to talk to Edmund. When the forks lay crooked, she straightened them. She helped carry salads into the banquet room and made sure all the menus went back up front. She asked Roz if she needed anything and then made cappuccinos and an espresso for her friend.

When they closed, Amanda told the others, no no no I'll do it, you go home I'm waiting for my roommate, and she chained all the café tables herself and married the ketchups and mustards. The other girls looked over their shoulders at Edmund as they walked off arm in arm.

Amanda planned that when the cab let them off in front of her place, she would stand on the stoop and tell him she was sorry but, he was a great guy, but. He would then have to catch another cab and go home.

But when she was finally done, when only the bus boys were left to sweep and the managers to pace and inspect, Edmund again kissed her with such a swooning fervency that she was forced to reevaluate. She was too tired to deal with that much emotion. She might do it later or she might leave a note or nothing at all. She would tell him she was exhausted and speak to him tomorrow. She wouldn't let him get out of the cab.

He hailed a taxi and they got inside and he placed both of his arms around her. He kissed the top of her head and groaned as he did so. He groaned and groaned and groaned. They pulled up, and she turned to him and said she was exhausted. He said that was okay. He wouldn't bother her, and couldn't he just tuck her in and then leave?

No, really, she said. Then she looked at him and his head was rolling back, like a baby that would gurgle. His pupils seemed to lose symmetry.

Really, no, she said, and one of his pupils held her fixedly while the other twitched off to the side. He grabbed her hand and said please. His skin grew very white and red. There was a bubble on his lip.

Okay, she said, Okay.

He tried to carry her up the stairs, but only made one step and then set her down, laughing. He kissed her and then threw his arms up for joy. He shook his head quickly as if toweling his hair.

Amanda tried to keep her back to him as they continued up the stairs. She felt sinking sinking and worried that her roommate would be home.

"Hello?" she called from the doorway "Hello, Tiffany? Are you home?" When no answer came, she walked to the center of the living room and Edmund shut the door behind them. Amanda sighed. She stood for a moment in the center of the room with her back to him.

He went to kiss her and she took a step away.

He searched her face. He walked toward her with his arms slightly spread. His mouth formed to say something but only grunts came out. It was a look of panic. She thought he would burst. She thought she would kill him. She was overcome with a sense of her own cruelty. She scoured within for a place that wanted to be touched.

He made love to her with passion. He wetly kissed every inch of her throat and clutched her. He bit with the perfect amount of restraint. He filled her ear with his tongue. He pressed and kneaded. Edmund thought he would die of Amanda.

Later, he stayed where he was, to hold her. Amanda—she thought she would laugh. She thought of work and the beepers and the jostling and prodding and she thought it was so stupid she'd laugh, and then she thought of home and her mother. She wondered if her greatest moments were behind her, and there was Edmund over her, heavily, sweating, and she felt such revulsion that she shoved him away with both her arms and legs and stood up, naked, with her back to him. She wrapped her arms around herself.

"I'm leaving. I'm going home," she said. "I don't want to date you."

Edmund shifted where he sat but did not speak. Amanda groped about for her clothes. She pulled on her shorts and then her T-shirt. She lifted her hair as her head poked through to its place and then she flung herself on the bed and cried. He lay over her like he was protecting her from fire or cold or bombs. He held her so that her bawling would stop. He smoothed her hair. "Shhh," he said.

He knew she was mistaken.

Because his love is a mother's love. It is for her own good. It is with an urgency and perfection she cannot fathom.

She has no idea what it is to be horrible. Someday, she might be horrible, and then there is only one kind of love that can stand you. And no one will   ever   love her like that again.

NO SUCH ABSOLUTE

IT HAD BEGUN the night before. All night, as if a frame were ripped from the continuum. She would be drifting toward sleep, that delicious tenderness—and then a yank. She blamed it on hunger and ate cereal. She blamed it on stress and then thought of each muscle, attempted to breathe through her calves, her neck, her pores. But each time she fell, swimmingly, deeper, she jerked. And so she then accepted that this was now her rhythm. For the time being, this was the way of Ana's life—a hum and then a thud, or rather, a hum and then a scrape. With a thud there is a bottom, heaviness, resting. But the scrape—a shock of adrenaline, an interruption which is not an end, but chaos. And to conceive the thing, to remember that flowing moments were inter-rupted by shrillness, to remember it at all, was to bring it about.

She had not slept or she had slept the entire evening.

And again that afternoon. In the diner. The chicken soup had been the perfect chicken soup, with just a touch of oil, those tiny ragged hoops on each spoonful. The vegetables' exquisite density and the place was nearly empty and it was quiet and she forgot. And then her teeth scraped iron, rust, and the wince lasted a full minute.

She recalled it, sitting later on the edge of the fountain, and her face reconstructed the expression. She turned away as if she sat before something awful.

Ana did not like this cringing over nothing. It was a sign of weakness. It angered her the way Greggy angered her with those small circles on her back—comforting when what one needs to do is collect oneself. Soothing when what a gal should do is face the task and get on. Those circles—those were a shriek in the flow. In those moments, he repulsed her. His pathetic, womanish comfort.

Ana, the practical one. Ana, who never got colds and who knew allergies were a figment of the imagination. Who had actually willed her own hives away after an incident or two with shrimp. She had little tolerance for others' self-defeat. Sweater-wimps, who got so used to heavy clothes early in the season that they needed them daily—girls who cried over boys who never loved them anyway and worse, they who worried over what *might* happen.

Ana's coworkers were appalled at her summer job last year. She worked in a day-care center and they had a boy who, every chance he got, went sprinting through the hallways. They spoke to him sternly, took his cookies away, called his mother, and still, at some random moments—moments which corresponded only to his care-takers' relaxing—*bam* he was out in the hallway, yelling incomprehensibly, laughing uncontrollably. It was the laughing that pissed them off the most. The workers were half wide-hipped middle-aged women and half agile teenagers, and eventually they would trap him between some combination of leaps and stolidness. And then some-one would have to watch him and his little darting eyes, his little rising bottom, for the rest of the day. It seemed his goal to get them twice in one day, but that they were usually able to control.

It was Ana's fifth year at the day-care center, and they had given her, at the ripe age of twenty, her own room and included the sprinter. Be careful, warned Mrs. Ruhala waving her knotted finger, keep an eye on that one. Ana had been one of the agile leapers for a number of these occurrences. She had skillfully driven the sprinter into the wall of Mrs. Ruhala's hips. Mrs. Ruhala felt she was honoring Ana with a challenge as the youngest worker with her own classroom—not only that, but the sprinter as well.

Ana had had a different understanding. She understood that her fellow workers liked these little parties. They liked gathering themselves, these thick-and-sturdy women and narrow reaching girls, into the hallway while the rest of the children stood sucking their thumbs in the doors. That this was the only time their pulses quickened. Mrs. Ruhala herself liked playing the general, making plans of attack. "Elizabeth you watch Martine's group and Martine, you close off the far end." This was the only story they told when they got home. Ana knew they expected her to fail.

Ana did something brazen. She shut the door. June passed without incident. Mrs. Ruhala noticed. She said, "You can't do that. Children need air."

As a testament to Ana's hard work, there was a strand of black hair leaking from her rubber band. "The windows are open," Ana carefully explained.

"Open the door," Mrs. Ruhala said, over her shoulder, waddling with her grey legs one after the other to the audible sounds of nylon on nylon. She got quite a distance before she turned and added, "It's a fire hazard."

Ana came in with one of those accordion-like things people put at the top of stairs when they have babies. "He's old enough to open that anyway," Mrs. Ruhala said. The sprinter was now nearly seven. Ana showed that it took a good six seconds to unhitch the thing, plenty of time for an agile teenager to leap and gather small flailing limbs to her bosom. "It's a fire hazard," Mrs. Ruhala said, and Ana unhitched the thing again, in the same six seconds.

"Take if off," Mrs. Ruhala said. "I think he needs counseling. I think he has problems at home." She whispered this last part and tilted her thumb, glugging. Ana was disgusted and quit.

And yet here was Ana, fearing the heaves and bringing them on. Allowing the disturbance. She had been on a walk, thinking, all day. She was on the edge of a fountain. The rushing water and the not-too-distant traffic were distilling into sameness. These were the early days of spring and Ana wore her winter coat but wore it open, so that the breeze touched her throat while her arms were sweating. There was a problem with her muscles kinking, becoming solid, not aligned as well as usual. She was furious with Greggy. He had recently proposed.

Four years ago, he had stood on her stoop with his bicycle while his girl-cousin wandered off. A girl Ana knew from school, not really a friend, but a girl she knew well enough to make an introduction. His name was Greggy from Gregorio and he was a bit older and in college. He asked her if she wanted ice cream and she said she was too full. He asked her if she liked the air show and she said no and then he stood there. He stood there swallowing and she stood on the stoop with her arms folded waiting for him to go away. He was too skinny for her taste and short, and his smile had a tic in it.

And then the next week they rode by again, Greggy and his girl-cousin, and waved from a distance, and then she felt he was a coward as well. To ride by—a Filipino, from the islands themselves, who doesn't stop to chat, us talkers—how ridiculous. There would have to be a reason and that was clearly cowardice. But the third time, she realized he would never stop to chat unless *she* waved him over. And she was a little disgusted with the way he so easily accepted the changing of her mind. The way there was not the slightest touch of resistance to her hints. Oh, I'm so hot, she said, and it wasn't hot in the least, and he took her for a pop.

Greggy was a malnutritioned little runt, really, thin as Ana's pinkie. She had about thirty pounds on him and she herself was slim. He had no qualities of self-protection. When they argued, he never hung up, and when she did, all she had to do was stand by the phone and count to three. He never went home when she was grumpy. He remained patiently in the periphery. She looked left and he stood quietly to the right waiting for her to turn back. She might have been thoroughly rude, and he would apologize. If she married him, she would always be the bad one, always a little guilty.

And in Ana's shrieking flowing day there was both a sensual acuteness and a certain dullness. She had been walking into people. She had had one of those days where whenever she met someone on the sidewalk, she moved to the same side they did. Because she never met their eyes, she would switch to the left or gesture again to the right and be stuck in that awkwardness. She would laugh a stupid little laugh and wait for the person to walk around without having seen their face. She would hear their small, frustrated exhales. And yet, at moments, she swore she could hear the difference between the squeaks of cranes in the distance and the chugs of buses. She could tell adult voices from children, laughter from yells—all in the distant din. She had had the perfect soup, and now, on the edge of the fountain in the afternoon, she could still taste the salty broth and in one place on her lip, toothpaste. This, and then iron, rust. She felt she understood lightning. It had everything to do with tension.

Ana smoothed her coat beneath her and shifted a bit on the cement. The park was rather empty, just a couple of bums and teenagers playing hooky. She crossed her legs and put her chin on her hand. The teenagers were sharing a pack of cigarettes across the way. A boy held a pack toward a girl with one white, slim, tube sticking out.

Ana fell to musing. Her musing remained within a small fixed radius. She was sure that if she could relax and let her mind wander, the decision would be made unconsciously, would be ready and waiting for her when she returned. She exhaled as if to cool the perfect soup, and yet her thoughts could not escape that axis.

She traveled the tiny space between two images of Greggy.

One day, a few summers ago, she had left her job at the day-care to visit his job at the pet store. It had been busy. He had been flustered. A woman waved a pretzel-like doggy toy overhead and asked if they had it in softer material. Greggy's boss was asking, "Do you need quarters . . . I said do you need quarters . . . I'm leaving now do you need quarters?" while Greggy tried to answer a number of questions at once. Ana stood off to the side smoothing her hair, looking around, and somebody's dog urinated. The woman apologized for the animal and offered to clean it up, but Greggy insisted that it was okay, smiling weakly, and got the mop. Other people were waiting in line while he mopped. "It's okay, mum," he said with his accent, and Ana worried that the woman thought he'd called her mother.

Ana waited ten minutes and he was still too busy to speak to her. He would look up at her once in a while. He would say, "just one minute," pleadingly, but finally she could not stand it anymore, and left. For some time afterward, Ana would associate Greggy with the smell of urine, that weak embarrassed smile edging over his face, as if he'd done it himself.

The Tagalog word *bolero* has, of course, evolved from the original Spanish term for the musical form. A *bolero/a* is a practicer of something between charm and bullshit. It is closer to charm in that it does not necessarily have a negative connotation. It is a mode of flattery, understood by both speaker and listener to be designed for the listener's elevation. It is closer to bullshit in that it has no necessary relation to the truth. *Bola* supposes no such absolute. The ends are the listener's inflated sense of self. The desire of the *bolero* to bestow *bola* upon a particular subject is a compliment in and of itself. The issue of truth is irrelevant. There is only so much *bola* and so much time. Subjects are selected from infinite possibilities. This brings us to the opposite end of the two-point radius, Ana's other image of Greggy.

Now, nearly two years ago, she was at a party with many people from both her own and Greggy's crowd. All of her favorite people were there, save her very best friend, Victoria Singsing, who had been sent temporarily away to console a grieving relative. Victoria's boyfriend Cesar was there. He was one of the more popular young men of their set. He played soccer, was broad-shouldered, slim-hipped, and elusive enough to keep the desire for his company alive. He would make his jokes and be on his way, demonstrate his charms and disappear.

Ana was watching him. When he was between conversations, he was so antsy that his fingers curled and uncurled against his sides. He would make his way to groups and open the circle through some gesture of affection. He slung his arm over another boy his age, said something with a hand to the young man's chest until the kid lit up, and then Cesar left.

But usually, he spoke with girls. He said things quietly from beneath his bangs. He grinned. They had to lean in to hear things and then they punched him lightly in the arm. He had tremendous teeth. One girl—a girl with wavy hair and slow patient blinks—she didn't appreciate Cesar's conversation and folded her arms, and then he moved on and was speaking with another girl for too long. Her name was Kitty Tolentino. Everyone knew her. She was very pretty in a way that was far too crude for Ana's personal taste. She was plump and her sweaters were tight and her voice was a high-pitched whisper. Kitty and Cesar had to press their ears to each other's faces to be heard. Cesar's voice would fall when he was flirting. Kitty's was always weak. Ana knew that if Victoria were to learn how long Cesar spoke to Kitty and what it looked like, Ana herself would have to convey the information. Nobody else would tell. This was the first thing that set Ana on edge.

But it was when Cesar approached Ana herself that she became very irritable. He spoke in audible tones from a respectable distance. There was nothing the least bit male-female in his approach. She had watched him all night, baring his gleaming teeth to all the girls, from the most popular to the shyest and least desired. He had made Regina giggle. Regina had a thick scar from a harelip, and here he was with his cup of punch, asking Ana how she liked school. His punch was swirling because he couldn't keep still. He paid no attention to her answer. And then he was gone and back to Kitty.

Greggy asked Ana to dance. Ana said no she didn't want to dance and, "Greggy," she said, "you are a poor dancer anyway." And then he stood there with his still punch, turning red. Cesar radiated into Kitty Tolentino across the room. Greggy stood next to Ana for far too long. By the time he walked away, enough time had passed that this departure had no necessary relation to her insult.

But Greggy came back with Ana's mother. He walked upstairs to the chaperones' room, where the parents were reveling in their further-practiced *bola*, and brought back Ana's mother. Every kid in the basement straightened just a bit and Ana's mom, being honored as the only mother on the dance floor, lit up just like Kitty Tolentino. And then Greggy came back with his own mother and his aunt and eventually Ana was quite touched by all the blushing older women with their swaying black buns and Greggy's noble and reserved style. And Ana felt everyone was right when they said there are two kinds of men in this world.

Ana turned from the image of Greggy in the pet store to Greggy dancing with the glowing older women and back until she was completely disgusted with herself and then she fixed upon the people who had arranged themselves on the benches across from her.

She felt she was watching a play. She felt this because the previous scene, the teenagers with their cigarettes, had been replaced without transition, without perceptible exit or entrance, and because the people across from her were arranged self-consciously against each other like poor actors. They were also absurd-looking people.

The woman in the center was heavy and pale white. She had a taut smooth skin which usually belongs to thinner darker people. It was as if the extra chin were as natural a part of her body as the cheekbone or the hairless soft underneath of a forearm. She also had rolls in her cheeks. She seemed to be wrinkling in huge bunches rather than tiny folds, and her aging had gathered two bulging tubes of flesh which stretched and gleamed like muscles beneath her eyes.

It seemed the woman in the center was being comforted. She had light brown hair and glasses and there were two men angled against her from either side, much smaller people. One, on the right, was touching the top of his head against the top of her head. They were not actually in a position to lean, for one skull to feel the pressure of the other. From the left, the person had reached his arm over the woman's shoulders. He was quite small, and his whole body lifted with the gesture. His behind was not on the bench. The whole scene appeared resolutely uncomfortable.

Ana's eyebrows visibly bunched. The woman was speaking slowly and methodically, and Ana, over the rush of the water behind her, tried to tune in. The men on either side were nodding in agreement. For a moment, Ana felt she'd caught a thread, felt she'd heard "but, I…," the opening which would widen, through which the information would pour. But then Ana thought she

heard a language which was not English. It had the harsh conso-
nants of German but none of the rhythms. It was no language she
recognized. It was not Slavic or Romantic, or Germanic, not in any
family she could place. It did not sound like they were speaking a
language of Europeans. It was driving her crazy.

The small man from the right smoothed the hair of the woman.
Their expressions were all very serious and heavy. Ana thought of
moving to sit near them, but decorum subdued her. She could think
of no subtle way of getting near them. If she walked past, it could be
at a moment in which they were silent. She thought, then, that they
were speaking English. She saw that the woman was devastated.

Ana felt that if she only concentrated hard enough she could
catch that whipping tail, a thread of conversation, and she attempted this for some time. The woman shifted. She touched her head
against the man on the right and the one on the left was lifted awkwardly at an angle. Ana tried everything within her power to hear
from where she sat, and then she realized this was as silly and child-
like as when she had prayed for dolls to appear out of thin air. She
knew her only option was to take her chance and walk by as closely
and slowly as possible. Ana stood up and then her mind had wandered enough. She had been distracted enough to have the decision
ready and waiting for her. A constriction had burst, her thoughts
could go anywhere. If she didn't answer Greggy now, or if she said
no, he would only wait for her. She would be making the decision
for the rest of her life.

THE MIDDLE OF OCTOBER

CARL MOVED in approximations, near misses. He knocked things, fumbled. His skin was lightly blemished. He spoke at an angle toward his shirt. He was a teenager, decidedly awkward. This wasn't the only problem.

He had had two loves in his life. One was Mrs. Leestma, wife of the college football coach, and the other was Mrs. Epp, wife of somebody else. They both, on separate occasions, had been soggy with drunkenness and slung over his shoulder. They both had pressed their horrible breath to his face, and it was all that he knew, and he took it for what it was.

He worked at a summer lodge, at the desk at night, did it three years in a row, and the Summer Wives, they were the biggest drunks of all. If they rented cottages for the season, the women would often stay all week, while the husbands drove in and out of the city during the weekends. The Summer Wives' parties were the loudest and latest parties of them all. Smack dab in the middle of the week, and there they were in lawn chairs on the back porch with their smoke-deep voices and the clinking ice. They drank until they had to yell at somebody and swear. *Dorothy goddammit Dorothy.* And sometimes one of them would come with her blurriness to the night desk. "Excuse me, hon. What is your name? Okay, sweetie, Carl, we have a problem. It's very embarrassing." And then they who were half drunk would assign the lady who could barely stand to Carl's shoulders, and he would lug her home. Sometimes they walked along, and sometimes they said, "Oh, that kid. He's okay," and left the two of them alone.

It was these comings and goings of the city folk which gave Potuga High School its fall sourness. Every year the population of the little town on the lake tripled, then diminished. And every year, there were those who promised themselves: This year, I will be polite. I will tell them how to get bait, or discuss the state of the roads, but under no condition will I teach anybody's daughter to skip petosky stones or wonder if that man's wife is really tilting her hips at such a luxurious angle for me.

But there was always the poor girl who was stupid enough to be somebody's summer something-to-do, and some nice local boy who had had a crush on her all year. And when the fall came, the young people of Potuga turned back to each other with that small sourness, shame or indignity.

The parents of Potuga could hardly take the moral high ground. They made gestures, told their children not to go out at night and for the girls not to speak to those bored teens at all, but how could they enforce these vague rules? After all, they had moved there. Potuga was only a ten-year-old town, built up gradually after the war and built up by the vacations of the folk who came up from the city for the summer.

When you get down to it, the parents of Potuga made little attempt to contain their teenagers. They sat shaking their heads from the hillside porches, but the truth was that resignation was part of their character. They shook their heads with disapproval, but they did it with a grain of salt. Most of the locals had given up their farms. Potuga was a good place for a small pleasant house on the lake and part-time work maintaining the off-season homes.

These were people who had sold their farms at what was almost a comfortable profit. Who were they to judge? they, who had sold their great-grandfathers' land. They had let it go, not out of failure, but, well, some would call it laziness. Then again, it wasn't too long after the war, and in the case of Carl's family, and in a few other cases, they had lost their men or their men had changed afterwards, and who could blame them? Who would argue with widows or veterans?

Carl's sense of foolishness ebbed more slowly than most, who forgave and comforted each other by the Halloween ball. He hadn't dated local girls.

But then finally there was Marie. Her people were Finnish, and her eyes were narrow as a Chinaman's and her hair as straight, though it was white blond. Her eyes were the purest blue Carl had ever seen. She was so pale you could see a bit through her, see every time the blood rushed through to its place in her cheeks. Red splotches rose up from a kiss or exertion or embarrassment.

She was younger, fourteen while he was eighteen, but she was the youngest of many children and the last one at home, and her folks weren't too strict and they seemed to like Carl. They had sold their farm and moved down from Esconaba just before school started, and Carl had braced himself for all the distaste that fall always brought, but here it was the middle of October and they were still together. Marie's mother yelled, with her throaty accent, to be home by nine-thirty, and Carl and Marie ran out holding hands as the screen door fell closed. They could usually get away with an hour more.

With Marie, everything he was, was okay. He had told her things and she had smiled. He had told her of Marian, his sister, and how she was a handful and a bit crazy, but smart in the strangest way too. How one day, she just had to pile all things shaped like pens—all the pens and pencils and some of mother's make-up and a screwdriver with the handle broken, but only the broken one—how she had to pile all of these up in the exact geometric center of the living room. How she had carried her thick body (she was a big girl) with such rapid urgency. How the project had been so important to her, and there was nothing they could do to stop her or she'd become hysterical. Carl was nervous when he told Marie. His voice had wavered, but Marie had thought it was cute and laughed.

He thought of telling her all his horrible truths. Next would be that he was secretly relieved that his father was dead—he hadn't known him—because he didn't want to be a farmer. And then maybe Mrs. Leestma. Carl hadn't really done anything. Just stood there while she draped herself over him. All things gradually, in progression.

Four things made Carl want to propose. The first was the Unpleasant Kiss Contest, which Marie won with that stiff lower lip covered with saliva, and the upper rolled in against her teeth. The second and third were the bus they took to the city that Saturday for shopping and lunch. In the restaurant, Marie turned the sugar upside down over her pasta because she thought it was parmesan cheese and then laughed like it didn't matter. On the way back, the bus was very crowded and Carl stood over Marie while she shared a seat with a mother and two small children. One of the kids fell asleep against Marie, just leaned over and nuzzled into her softness, and Marie was so moved, an expression of begging for mercy flashed over her face. The fourth and most overwhelming fact was the way Marie's ankle curved into her calf. She said yes. They had, as of yet, told nobody.

Marie had wanted to know why he had met her family three times and she had only waved at his mother from a distance. Okay, Carl said.

If only it had just been Marian that day. If only his mother had not been sick as well. She had not been sick in many months, and so Carl was sure it would be okay. It usually came in spurts, months of migraines, and then months of peace.

At first when it had begun, six years earlier, Carl tried to take over the housework. He was able to do the most important things —he cooked, did laundry and minded Marian. But he soon discovered that even if he worked morning to night, he could not do all the undone, and that if he just waited for the months to end, Mrs. Morstock would return to her senses and attack.

When she was sick she simply left a trail all day. She could shut no door. It was enough to have opened the bathroom cabinet or kitchen drawer or refrigerator, and her mouth hung stupidly open with the effort. Her arms hung to the side and she left things as they were. She dropped her clothes everywhere. She shuffled, moaning. She got half way through cooking and gave up. Burgers floated in grease. Potato peels curled where they would. Carl constantly checked the gas just in case. She strung toothpaste, and make-up fell out of her hands to rest where it landed on the floor. She came mumbling out of the shower with her hair half lathered.

By the end of her bad months, the entire house would be as sticky as egg whites, and Carl, try though he might, he could never locate the source of the smells. When Mrs. Morstock was better, she would find it. She would go on a cleaning spree with her embarrassed smile and keep it that way. Squeaky scrubbing, linoleum sparkling.

He tried a few times, during her months of illness, tried to keep the drawers shut and the caps on and the contents placed, but eventually he relinquished his efforts and kept to the basics—Marian, dinner, the laundry, and things that stink or are disgusting. He found insects squashed against the bathroom mirror. He found a bowl of cereal under his mother's bed with the milk curdled and rank.

Such would not be the case for Marie's visit. For Marie's visit, Mrs. Morstock was free and clear. They planned for days, and although he felt it would be too much to use it for such a simple occasion, Carl even polished the silver in case it was seen. He beat the rugs on the back porch and straightened the pictures on the wall. Mrs. Morstock had him help pick out her dress. She emptied the couch of pocket change and mopped with resolve. She arranged lilacs in a vase.

He had left plenty to do that day, so that he wouldn't go crazy with waiting. The two houses to the left were summer homes which Carl maintained. He left his weekly visits until the morning of Marie's dinner. It was a Saturday. He fixed a loose tile and put down some pesticide. He mowed the Morstock's own hillside lawn and it made him sweaty, so he showered, knowing he'd do so again soon. His mother sent him to the butcher's for a duck.

He should have known from the way they were at the butcher's. Everyone was moody and irritable—the butcher, his son, his wife who was also the cashier, and most of all, the customers. There was no reason for Mrs. Vlasin to exhale impatiently through her nose, she was next up, and the butcher's wife would bang the drawer shut with her hip, drumming her fingers. Carl distinctly saw the son look coldly and angrily into his butcher-father's eyes and the father look callously back. As he walked out, as Carl folded the paper a little better over the slimy bird, as he ran his fingers over the package searching for the tied-up feet, he looked up at the sky for a storm but there was nothing.

When he got home, he opened the door gradually with his shoulder like an unannounced visitor. "Mom?" he called gently, around the corner into the kitchen. She was in there roasting pumpkin seeds, moving determinedly about and smoothing her hair.

"I figured we could eat these while the duck is finishing up. I'm running behind schedule," she said a bit nervously, and Carl sighed. She pulled a tray of the browned seeds out of the oven and placed another tray inside. She poured the first batch into a bowl and said, "Here, are you hungry? Have yourself a snack."

He took his bowl out to the front porch and took Marian with him. He showed her how to spit seeds into her fist and then thought, perhaps it was not so attractive to have people spitting shells on such an important occasion. Oh, but then again, everything he was, was okay. Even Marian was okay in her hugeness—she was such a big girl, such a thick middle on spindly legs. Even Marian with her vapid glare. She smiled lovingly at Carl and he hugged her. She spit a shell into her fist and then held out her open hand with the evidence and beamed. They had the same dark brown hair and green eyes. The same pinched tip of their noses.

Carl heard a noise. It sounded like rattles, and he wondered for a moment if it weren't in his veins, and then he walked inside, opening the door slowly. "Mom?" he said, around the corner, and there she was. The tray was still in her hand. She still held the thing with her kitchen mitt, but loosely by the corner, and the pumpkin seeds were all over the floor and her mouth hung stupidly open.

"Oh, Mom," he said. And he was afraid she would burn her knees with the hanging tray, so he wrapped a kitchen towel around his hand and took it from her. He had to hold her by the arm while he pried her fingers open.

"No, no, no. I'll do it. No, no, no. It's okay." There was nothing he could do to hide his disappointment, but there was no way Mrs. Morstock could continue either. He heard her fumble to the bathroom for her medicine with that rattling sound of spilling things and then into her room with a low moan. He called Marie to cancel but she wasn't home, and having two and a half hours left, he figured he could come up with something himself.

Carl did the best he could. He had no idea what to do with a duck, but he didn't make a bad meatloaf and knew precisely how much to burn macaroni. He was very nervous. His hands shook and he was sweaty. He grew conscious of every place his body touched itself. His armpits, his privates, and his calves against his thighs as he squatted to the lower cabinets looking for pans. He became quite damp.

His first trip to the grocery, he had to bring Marian. It was just a few blocks, but it wouldn't be right to leave her there with his mother sick and unable to watch. She had been known to do dangerous things. Carl had seen her placing the tips of her fingers in the face of the fan.

But she slowed him down and time was of the essence. He had decided to walk quickly and force her to follow and keep up. She was a few paces behind him with her mass and her skinny legs flinging this way and that. She kept calling his name: "Carl, Carl." This was during the time Marian became obsessed with stop signs. Every time she saw a stop sign she was sent into convulsions of euphoria. She clasped her hands against her open mouth and bounced. "Carl, Carl," she called, pointing at the stop sign. She pointed, then covered her mouth, pointed, then covered her mouth. Carl grabbed her by the hand and pulled her down the hill.

The second time, he knew it wasn't the right thing to do but he had no time. He had forgotten raisins. *Marian,* he said, with all the urgency he could muster, *Marian, do not move from this chair. No matter what. If someone rings the bell. If you hear any noise besides me, don't move do you understand?* He had her wrists tightly in his hands and the way that he squeezed must have told her too. She seemed to understand. She seemed to be excited by an idea of such importance, by having a mission.

This time, the girl in the grocery, the cashier, it was as if her greatest thrill in life were to make people wait. She had this screwed-up, cruel little face. Her name was Helene Patterson and Carl knew her from Trigonometry. She turned items over to look at the bottom. She whistled. She paused to place a finger on her chin and think. Carl had always hated her. All Carl had was a simple box of raisins, and the lady in front of him had one of every kind of fruit there is. One after another in the scale, a pomegranate, for God's sake, one banana, one pear. Carl shook with frustration and then sprinted home, cursing Helene. Marian was where he had left her.

He decided to shower before he finished dinner; better to be mid-cooking, but clean when Marie arrived. Mrs. Morstock had left her trail in the bathroom. Her big white pills were strewn all over the sink, the cap on one side of the room, the bottle on the other, the cabinet open. The towels had been pulled off the rack and even the toilet paper was half unwound. He shoved things into place as quickly as he could. He showered and then checked on his mother and her low moan. He brought her ice and stroked her head a few times.

He poured the raisins into his mix and formed the loaf and then it was close to time, so he checked out the window, looked up the road with his hands still thickened with grease. Not yet. He placed things in the oven. Washed his hands, and there was Marian in the corner, drooling. *Wipe your mouth*, he said with that sternness—a sternness he didn't usually use—and Marian went to wipe with the back of her hand but he shoved her a napkin. He felt a rush of panic. He felt himself contract in toward the center like a sprung trap.

He had an idea. He had his new sternness. He took Marian by the wrist to her room and sat her on her bed and held her with the same urgency as before. *Don't move from here until I tell you.* He said and it seemed to work. She had a bubble on her lip and he rubbed it off with his thumb.

Carl washed dishes. His mother softly cried, and then the house was silent. Carl washed a dish and then checked out the window, washed a dish and then checked again.

He had a thought and went back to look at Marian. He rummaged through her drawer and found a bra. *My God. Put this on.* And she began to unbutton her shirt to do what was ordered.

Marie came up the hill in a purple sweater. Carl marveled at the way her pale feet swooshed, one then the other, at the way her eyes pulled taut her skin. Her smile opened to full capacity an instant behind his own.

He said hello with a choke in it. She looked puzzled for an instant and then went back to her smile.

He pulled out a chair for her at the table. It was at the end, the seat he could see from the kitchen. He pulled on his kitchen mitts. "Mom started to feel sick, so I'm just finishing up for her."

"Is it a bad time?" Marie asked. "Should we set another day?"

Carl spoke toward his shirt and Marie had to ask him to repeat himself. "No, no, she went to all this trouble."

Marie felt ridiculous with him in the kitchen and insisted that he let her finish. All there was to do was set the table and wait on the meatloaf. He showed her where the silverware was. They only set two places.

They sat waiting. Carl was huddled. He leaned forward then back. He tried to make small talk. He could see, out of the corner of his eye, the expressions ripple over Marie's face. There was confusion and then disgust.

Carl exhaled in pulses and looked at his hands. Marie seemed about to say something and then said nothing.

Marian came out with her broom. Marian came ripping out with her broom and her bright idea. She had her tongue curled up to the side of her face with the deliciousness of her idea. She had on her bra, but her shirt bunched up on top where the straps were absurdly twisted. In one hand she had the broom and in the other she had a piece of paper she had crayoned in red. She was throwing her spindly legs in a near run. Her body was bouncing.

Carl did not have to look. He could sense Marie's shock from where he sat. Hadn't somebody told her? Surely somebody would have told her by now.

Marian made it to the kitchen and went rummaging through the drawer. She found the scissors and cut off the corners of her red paper so that it was a hexagon, then taped it to the bristle end of her broom and ran out and said, "Carl, look, look." Marian held up her project, her fingers worming excitedly together as she leaned the whole thing against her huge soft chest. Her tongue curled to the side of her face.

"She likes stop signs." Carl was imploring.

He walked his sister gently back to her room, a hand to the small of her back.

Marie was very polite while they ate, just the two of them. She said it was good. Her voice was softer than it had ever been. Carl's fork panicked against the plate and in mid-air, so that he dropped food he'd attached to it. It took concentration to swallow.

Once, his mother called his name in her suffering voice. It was a horrible, breathless, suffering voice. He had to leave Marie alone at the table for a good five minutes.

After he returned, they could hear Mrs. Morstock's low moan, and their eyes rolled off as it happened but they stayed sitting.

Marie cleared the dishes but did not wash them and Carl went to Marian and told her under no condition to move and walked his date home.

On the corner of her lawn, he said, "I thought someone told you."

"I thought your sister was a little girl."

"We're twins."

Marie started to cry and he went to kiss her, leaned to within inches and then thought better of it and turned and walked home. He knew, but he could not help himself. He called one more time and she made herself clear.

PROMISE

VICTOR'S OWN TRAINER named him Kid Candlelight. The lights would go out on him, every time. 0 in 9 when he quit, a big hulking loser of a kid. Cruiserweight at sixteen, six-foot-two, one hundred and ninety-one pounds. In the last bout, half the spectators yelled for Victor's opponent to drop the knife. He bled that much.

And to this very day there's evidence. No cartilage in the bridge and one nostril crawling up on an angle. Not that that's a problem. He's not ugly. Women still like him. He's tall and sharp-dressed with only a slight belly, and he knows how to be the gentleman.

He loves to tell the stories. He laughs. He can laugh, now, because he understands the reasons and he forgives himself for blowing that shot. There was marijuana, and Marlene, and a couple of guys—buddies he used to run with until all hours of the morning.

When Victor showed his promise, his own father had been so excited, his father had seen Victor as a man and lifted his own glass to him and let him run all hours of the night and party and be beamed at by girls who thought he had a chance too. Victor lost his concentration, that acuteness that they knew meant he had it in him. He lost his discipline to premature glory, fell apart.

He had been very promising. They had thought they could make a boxer out of him because he was fast and accurate for a kid of his size. They had seen him in practice, coming into this state of mind. He would narrow his eyes and there would be one thing he wanted, and he was quick and powerful when he sparred. He choked in public. He could never enter that state, never tune. The trainer was sure he would get over his stage fright, until about 0 and 6 and then he threw up his hands and said, "Kid Candlelight," a bit under his breath but loud enough that it was overheard.

There would be so many things to think about that Victor couldn't think at all, and when he finally got Marlene pregnant, Victor himself knew he did it half on purpose. A good excuse to be needed for something else.

Now Victor owns a diner and other small businesses. He makes so much money that last month he went to Puerto Rico for lunch. He told his wife he was going fishing, got to the airport at dawn, met a lady in Old San Juan before noon, took her to a hotel, and even made it better than a quickie before turning around, landing at Kennedy, and having a late dinner at home.

He runs numbers. Which he doesn't have to feel guilty about. It doesn't hurt anybody except those who have it coming. Those who open a spot too close without checking, or workers who try to beat him, skim a little off the top. These people know what they're doing when they do these things. Even so, he has never tried to make anybody truly suffer. He just did what was necessary. He has destroyed businesses, but not people. Even when he found the woman from the laundry was taking him for two or three a week, all he did was fire her.

Victor sells chances and luck. He doesn't steal personal property or make people sick with addiction. Not like the young men on this block. His diner's block. They know him here. The young men on this block, always there. The young men, selling crack cocaine or guarding crack cocaine or just hanging out. Victor is not in the business of drugs, though he dabbles himself just a bit for distraction. Always there, those kids on the corners, in front of the businesses, the video store with a handful of tapes, the record store with old disco albums, the grocery with thirty rolls of the exact same brand of yellowed paper towel. Sitting on cars or talking on pay phones (business), or talking to girls where their mothers can't hear. And at night the girls are there too.

The other day, when Victor was closing up at two, just before he pulled down the gate in front, he saw a dozen kids wander into the neighborhood. Or try to look like they wandered, because there has to be a reason a dozen strangers come into the neighborhood and spread out over the street and look at all the stoops and corners and puff out their chests, but still look for each other in the periphery to know they're not alone. A dozen fifteen-year-olds, mostly skinny, walking purposefully, slowly. The one in front—he took a last drag on his cigarette. He was squinting and he held the thing between pointer finger and thumb. Then he dropped the butt and stepped on it and turned quietly towards the projects and the others followed with their eyes sweeping the streets, watching with as wide a scope as possible.

When they disappeared behind the buildings, the streets were almost empty of girls and the young men were standing together in a few larger groups. They gathered from the pay phones and stoops and corners and hoods of cars and stood only in three places, in front of the bodega and the record store and the first sidewalk that winds into the projects.

Victor's keys were the loudest thing on the street as he locked the door behind him.

The next few days he asked around, but the only thing he heard was that four days later they found a junkie's body in the dumpster. It was only a junkie, but still, there must have been family.

Tonight was a terrible night. There were a number of hits and all that's left is seven worn hundreds. Victor palms these sad bills and tucks them away.

George from the hospital is trying to beat him. Not skim a little off the top, but massacre Victor's livelihood, take him for all he's got. George from the hospital was doing great business, collecting numbers from his fellow-workers, from the neighborhood. He pulled in twelve thousand a week for a thirty-five-percent cut. Victor gave him an extra large cut. And then he starts getting hits for nine or ten every other week. Yesterday Victor told him, be here no later than 7:45, but George came in at 8:03, after the race started. Victor didn't have the second number yet, all he had was 5. If George had someone at the track, he could have gotten a call before he stepped in the door and said sorry he was late.

Victor had 5-2-. . . by 8:06, and wouldn't you know, George had between seven and seventy-three dollars on every 5-2 combination.

Luckily it was 5-2-8, which paid only seven thousand. If it had been 5-2-1, Victor would have owed nearly sixty thousand dollars.

George must be stupid. No one has ever attempted this kind of devastation before. Its obviousness is hateful.

Victor always has a last cigarette at the window, watches the street before he pulls the gate down. This is usually his delicious moment of quiet. He sits and puts his feet up on another chair. But tonight, this George thing makes his temples throb.

And then three of his spots have been shut down in the last two weeks. Each time he had to bail the guy out and pay a fine. And three spots is starting to look like someone is putting it all together or giving information. Spots get hit all the time, but not three in two weeks. Sometime soon, they'll hit the office again, and he'll have to destroy paperwork and spend the night in jail.

Sitting there in the dark with his cigarette, Victor thinks he might be losing it. A rush of panic overtakes him. The police and the numbers and George and the hospital and the laundry—it makes him dizzy and for a moment he's not sure his limbs will go the way he directs.

He takes a deep breath and calms himself with Bernadette. Bernadette is the biggest thing. She is the one. She is eight years older than him, a sophisticated woman. They've been at it for half a decade. She quit him for a year in the middle. She is married too. Bernadette's children are older and out of the house and her husband runs around at night. When the husband calls to say he won't be home until late—meaning tomorrow, he has business to take care of, a friend from out of town—Bernie says okay and calls Victor. He closes up by two and they meet in an after-hours club.

Bernadette drinks scotch like a man. Johnnie Walker Red, straight up. She laughs in all the right places. She waits for half an hour, and if Victor is later than that, she leaves. And then she won't call him for a month. She can call him at work, but she herself does not work and there's no telling when her husband is home. Victor has to wait until she's done being angry.

She has recently forgiven him. And tonight, Victor will meet her at three and have two drinks and then kiss her. He wants to take her lower lip between his teeth. Not bite, just hold her lip there gently for a moment and show that he can be trusted. She has the blackest sleekest hair, and he'll kiss her and slide the pins from the back of her head and cool his hands on her hair as it falls.

Victor butts out his cigarette, rests a moment in the peace of the closed-down diner. The outside noises, the yelling and the radios and the honking, have settled into a hum. And the diner, its grease and the clanking and the constant phone—in the dark it's all gone.

It's Bernie's eyes though. Bernadette has light eyes. Bernie Bernie Bernadette who has almost forgiven Victor for the last offense, who will meet him at three o'clock. She is a dark woman with eyes much lighter than her skin. They come out gold, tiger-colored, and they're big, and when he apologizes and sits in the quiet and takes her hand and waits for what she'll say, every simple blink will be a stoking.

Victor washes his hands. He checks the mirror and smoothes the hair over his ears one last time. He steps outside, grabs the top of the metal gate, rises on his toes a bit to get ready for a good smooth yank and hears some footsteps and looks over his shoulder and it's a young girl he knows and she says hello.

"Hello, Miss Lucia," he says. She is a young girl with a crush on him. She hovers and smiles, looks at the sidewalk. "Where are you coming from at this late hour?"

She shrugs deeply. Lucy loves Victor. He's kind to her. He asks after her mother and remembers the things she says. *Did you get over your allergies? Did you enjoy the movie? That deadbeat uncle of yours is still around?* He remembers she doesn't like her eggs runny and reminds the cook as soon as she walks in the door. Her mother plays 2-0-5, Lucy's birthday, and Lucy is sent with a couple of dollars on days her mother feels lucky. They hit a couple of months ago and her mother bought Lucy rollerblades.

Lucy is stacked. Curvy is not even the word. She's like a twisted balloon. Waist and wrists and ankles of a tiny child and hips out to here and breasts underwire is having trouble containing. Pow. Boom. A body like that is a tragedy on a girl like Lucy. Her face has remained for years in the height of the awkward stage. She might never come out. She has pimples and she plucked the inside half of her eyebrows so they sit four inches apart. What young men will do to a girl with a body that won't quit and a face like that.

Victor knows she has a crush on him. He thinks it's cute. She makes him feel generous, the way she lights up with his attention. This sweet sad child floating in blue jeans.

He was rising on his toes to yank the gate down and then go meet Bernadette.

"How was business this evening?" Lucy asks. She straightens her arms, hands deep in pockets. She rolls her head to her shoulder. Her hair is pulled tightly and smoothed with gel.

"Just fine, Miss Lucia. Okay." And while they're exchanging pleasantries and during the smallest most subtle bend that Victor makes before going up on his toes and again grabbing the gate to yank, something happens around them.

A group of men Victor's age and slightly younger walk very quickly towards a big brown sedan. Somehow, too fast for seeing, they open the doors. Then they lean against the open doors and the bumper and push the car a body's length forward. They do not start the engine.

Next to Victor's diner, there is a fenced-in parking lot with the door chained shut. The brown sedan had been blocking the tall wire door of the fence. Someone undoes the chain clang-clang-clang and pulls the big gate back. A truck comes along with a little blue sports car in tow. The truck swings through the space where the sedan was and enters the parking lot. And then, while this is happening, behind the choreography, a van pulls up. And so one guy rushes over and holds up his hand like a traffic cop. You can see the van driver at first look nervous and then hang his wrist over the steering wheel and shift impatiently. The truck backs out without the blue sports car and takes off and then they let the van go. The chain is slid back through the fence. The sedan is pushed back where it was.

Lucy looks to Victor and he's reaching up for that gate and then one more thing happens. Somebody starts throwing gravel. Maybe a kid. Little kids do things like that. It ricochets all over the walls, pelting enough so that Lucy bows and covers her face. One of the guys from the cars stops and looks up to see where the gravel is coming from. By the time he looks up, it stops, but he keeps look-ing up. It could come from a window across the street and it could come from the building above Victor. The man is looking up and up to figure it out.

It's not even that—it's when the other men look back at this last one and make an agreement in one quick nod. One more will stay behind, and the two of them will be the ones to take care of this gravel problem. Another stops walking, and the two of them scan the roofs and upper windows. They have their eyes narrowed like the last hard hit of a cigarette. That is when Victor forgets the gate and tells Lucy to get inside.

Victor makes Lucy stand in back of him at the door, his arm over her chest like a mother driving. He is very bulky and blocks most of the doorway. He watches for a second as the two men scan upwards, gripping something in their jackets, and then Victor decides it's better not to watch and turns to Lucy and says, "We'll just wait here for one moment." They stand next to each other, without talking, like an elevator, and then Lucy braces herself.

It is not a coincidence that Lucy passes by as he is locking up. She's got things she's planned to say to Victor, who would guard her from gravel and worse in the street. She's nervous. Her adrena-line is betraying her, and she might cry if she speaks. She had a plan when she came here and she just must take a breath and say it. "I have something for you, Victor."

"What is it, Lucy?" He glances out to see if they can leave yet.

Bernadette.

The two men are still combing, their hands in their coats.

Lucy produces a square pocket mirror in purple rubber casing. She dips her pointer finger in the casing and slides out a razor blade.

"All right, come here." Victor locks the front door quickly and then leads her by the elbow to the office where they cannot be seen. He locks that door too. If he does blow, he'll fuck her. Victor knows this. Lucy with stubble for half her eyebrows. He's calculating the time before he'll meet his real woman. It won't be so bad. Bernie will wait a little while. And if he does a couple of lines, he'll be able to make Bernadette listen like she should. He'll be confident, say what needs to be said.

Victor takes the hand-held mirror and lays it on the desk. He reaches out so that Lucy can give him the cocaine. She puts her little folded paper in his palm.

It's nothing. Damn, it's not enough. Perhaps, if Victor did this entire quantity by himself, he might get off. Stupid girl saving her pennies for this pathetic seduction. Victor could give it back, or he could cut her a measly portion. She could probably get off on a thin little piece of shit. Victor checks his disgust. He doesn't say anything but the sigh of frustration cannot be helped, and when he does this, it's not like Lucia doesn't notice. She curls her back, with those breasts, as if to compensate. Victor sighs one more time for resignation. This is silly. He's thinking of time and getting it over with and maybe getting some more blow on the way to meet his lady friend. He opens his desk drawer and pulls out a bottle of White Label. He pours two shots in plastic cups and toasts Lucy.

"Salud."

"Salud."

Victor pours two more and warms his stomach. He cuts himself two thirds and does it quickly. Lucy does her thin line and giggles.

Nothing. This produces nothing, and Victor pours another shot, leans against the desk with a far away look.

Lucia has been dumped by a boy who now hates her. Victor can save her. Victor has been very kind to her for a long time. He asks after her mother. Very polite. This is a kind-hearted man. But his mood has changed. She has got to do something. She steps closer, everything about her body offering itself, shoulder blades pinched, head rolled back so that she's all breast and neck. The air goes tender around them. He could lift a breast slightly with his knuckles. Victor pours another shot. Victor can be good to this girl.

He fucks her kindly, simply. This is a girl that boys fuck to say they've fucked her. Acrobatically, steering by that tiny grippable waist. I did this and then I did that. But Victor, he isn't like that. He's all fingertips and air. When it's over, he pours a double shot and then another.

He wakes just before dawn on the office couch. The girl's face is on his chest. Her hair is greasy with gel against his skin and his own breath tastes rotten. He wakes to a chilly, sour hangover.

He reaches for his underwear. He shakes Lucy.

"Sweetie, we gotta go." Lucy rubs her eyes, sits for a moment and stares.

"Hurry up," he says, without looking, and to save time he runs to the bathroom while she's dressing. He brushes his teeth, smoothes his hair. His face is flushed and red and he'll have to think fast and be sharp. He can't do it with the girl there. He'll think in the car.

Bernadette. And then if she abandons him he'll be depressed and unbearable for months just like last time and his wife will threaten to go too. And then his kids will always be cringing like he's some kind of monster.

On the way to the girl, on the way to hurrying her out, he pats his pockets for the seven soft hundreds in the money clip, and they're not there. He checks all his pockets, left breast, right, pants front and back, twice, again. The money is not there. He looks on the desk. He moves things, stacks of papers, the ashtray. He puts away the bottle of White Label, throws out the cups, wiping lipstick away with his thumb. He checks the floor, beneath the cushions of the couch. The girl stands waiting by the door.

"You seen my money?"

She says she hasn't seen his money. He looks out by the door where they stood hours ago. He looks out front under the gate. He looks in the bathroom, the counter, the floor. He gets down on his hands and knees and checks under the sink, behind the toilet. His head is pounding and he has to breathe carefully to keep from throwing up. His palms and knees are damp and that disgusts him. He finds the girl dressed, watching hesitantly near the front door.

He curses Lucy. He digs his thick fingers into her arm, pulls her into the office and stuffs those same thick fingers into the cups of her bra, and then he makes her take her clothes back off, stand with her bare feet on the grimy office floor. She's sobbing.

"You took my fucking money."

"I didn't take your money, Victor," and then she says, "I swear," and that cements it. He searches every crevice of her clothes, the whites of her pockets, her socks. He turns the lining of her panties out.

"You took my fucking money." He finds nothing, throws her clothes at her. "I don't know where you put it." He's tempted to throttle this girl. She's hysterical, all mucous and gasping. Arms over her head, like he might hit her when he would never do that, when he's not even like that. "Get the fuck out of here."

"I didn't do it," she moans and snorts and pleads and runs with her fat face out the door. Her red eyes and pimples and her smeared runny nose.

Victor's mouth is coated. His headache is shrill. He'll drive by Bernie's place and see if her husband's car is on the street. He'll say he was in jail. He'll tell her he loves her, cry if he has to. He'll buy a dozen roses on the way. He'll tell her about George and she'll feel for him. If she lets him make love to her he will give to every single surface of her body. He'll take her to San Juan for lunch. If her husband is home, he'll wait until a decent hour and then get his cousin, the girl, to call and ask for Bernadette. If her husband answers, he won't suspect a thing. Victor's cousin will pretend to want to go shopping, and set up a meeting.

But the money. The damn money. He hasn't a cent on him and he'll have to pass by his house or wait until seven for his partner to show. He'll need money for flowers and a hotel. Victor throws his weight into a chair to sulk and decide. The answer will come to him. Bernadette will say okay, okay and put her slender fingers to his lips. His headache pounds. Everything smells like bleach. He grips his own skull.

Three years ago, when Bernie quit him before, he couldn't sleep and he became irritable and started to hate his wife's ways. The way she breathed in the morning. The peach fuzz on the back of her hand, the way she punctured peas before she ate them. He told her to fucking stop that. She got him aggravated, and she answered, "So leave." And the kids sneered and folded their arms.

Victor's sour, bleached headache.

Bernadette. Everything crumbling around Bernadette. He must look a wreck, and he walks to the mirror and when he's doing that, he feels an extra softness to his step and wouldn't you know, the seven worn hundreds must have fallen to the bottom of his sock.

So now he rushes and straightens himself. He left the gate up all these hours and thank god nothing happened to his diner. He yanks the gate down. He goes rushing for his car. He parked five blocks away in a better neighborhood for cars. Funny how there is the feeling of dew in the morning on this street with no trees. He'll take her earrings out with his mouth. She'll be angry and scream at first, and then after he pleads, she'll say okay, shhhh and rub his head.

Victor goes sprinting for his car, and in his shape, walking quickly is not even easy. He walks like a madman, like a force beyond his control shoves his legs one after the other, and the rest of his body wobbles and can barely keep up. He's sprinting, huffing and puffing and nauseous and dreaming of comfort. The spill of her hair.

What she'll want is convincing. As much as she'll hate him, she'll want to be made to believe. He has done this before in crucial moments in his life.

Back before he was Kid Candlelight, when he absolutely knew he had it in him, Marlene was a pretty girl just a little younger than Lucy. Her cheeks were full and smooth. Young men came to her with gifts. She wasn't like Lucy. She wasn't the girl young men yelled at from their cars. Marlene was the one they turned up their radios for. They hoped she'd look and then they'd pose with their toughness and their property. Victor was a boxer and she believed in him. Tears lined her lower lids and he touched them away with the crook of his finger. He cupped her face, palms to her chin and fingertips to her ears, like thirst. A canteen or a chalice or a gourd. He pulled her close and meant what he said. Lips just short of a kiss, he said Baby I will. We can. I promise. He said, Baby I can save you. Baby be strong. He said, baby, baby, baby.

He could do this for Bernadette, drink from her face and make her believe. He jumps in his sleek little car and starts the ignition, and in a way he knows he's got it in him. He can be sharp and grip the loose and scuttling ends. But then again, he's bracing himself for the worst. He's started over before, and he knows how it is, and he expects to be miserable and survive.

THIRTY SECONDS

THOSE THIRTY SECONDS determined the rest of his life. And the controlling mechanism, the driving force behind the decision which directed this life to come, was a fear of his own capacity for degradation.

He stood there with his finger on the reset button, an other-wordly panic raging through his veins. And then he made the call. The undoable. He stood there with his finger on the reset button and made the decision to do the undoable. He could not help himself. There was no other decision to make. He wanted it over with. He wanted never to experience that sensation again.

He was thoroughly convinced of his own sickness, and had to act.

Colonel Bobby De Los Santos, the Handsome. This is what they called him, the Handsome. He had made his way in the world because of it. He was forty-seven, and still women touched him on the elbow as he passed, complete strangers, looking him full in the eyes, giving him the go ahead—*Come for me.* They did this still, as they'd done since he was a teenager, as if they were the first and the only with the bright idea.

His face configured closely to popular depictions of the ideal and yet differed enough to be unexpected, unnerving. Jaw, broad; eyes, tilting and pinched like half sleep.

He had stopped by Megamall to buy a wallet for himself and one for his cousin's birthday. He had ridden with the chauffeur. He didn't feel like driving. In the parking lot, he saw his wife get into the passenger seat of Doro Melendez' car. Doro had a hand to the small of her back. His wife was laughing.

It was silly, really. Doro had been a friend of the family all along, practically a cousin to Isabel. Their mothers were friends, they were raised together. But Bobby—a force beyond control was operating, and he was without doubt, he had complete surety, they were heading to his house for an afternoon tryst.

It was completely impractical. It was not at an hour in which they could expect privacy, but Bobby was convinced of the whole scenario. He told the driver to take a detour which would allow them time to take their clothes off. He wanted to catch them undeniably. He would put his gun to Doro's head. He would not kill him, but terrorize him. He would make Doro stand and walk, naked. He would have both righteousness and, yes, a bit of madness on his side. Doro was a general, and Bobby would later continue, business as usual, taking orders, but they both would know who feared whom.

And so they drove, and Bobby forced himself to imagine every detail so that he could correctly time the entrance. His wife being coy, as she had, long ago, during the initiation of romance, been apt to be. This button. This hesitation. The giggling.

Isabel De Los Santos was not a beautiful woman. She was good-looking, yes, but she was not a head-turner as Bobby himself was, and yet she felt she could control people. She flirted as if she had all the power in the world and this quality, this surety of her own nonexistent beauty, this Bobby had admired when they first came together, and now it infuriated him. Her skin was slack. Her neck was too short, and yet she carried herself like a perfect specimen and they all were fooled.

Bobby De Los Santos, his rage rising, his otherwordly rage, and he concentrated, he forced himself to rein it in so that he might concentrate.

They pulled up, Bobby signaled with a wave of the hand that the driver should wait in the car. The driver—he tried, he knew it was his duty to contain all expression, but the colonel knew he knew. He had seen Isabel and Doro as well.

He would need the utmost of silence to really catch them in the act. He removed his shoes before he even put his keys to the lock. The metallic click irked him, but then everything was perfect. He pushed open the door smoothly with his shoulder, one hand on his holster. He tiptoed across the marble, set his shoes by the stairs. He was breathing deeply, but with amazing control. As long as everything was even, steps, light, not too swift, even his heartbeat—and then he flew with the bedroom door in one hand and the other on his hip, his gun.

And they were not there and he flew to the bathroom in his stocking feet, with that precision of step, and threw open the shower curtain, and then back to the master bedroom to check each closet, to no avail, and then—it would be laughable later—the space under the sink in the bathroom, and then the other bedrooms, his daughter's, the guests', their bathrooms, the linen closet—how absurd, as if they could fit in the shelves—the little house out by the pool, and when he finally stopped, was when he ran into the servants' rooms.

There was Loling, the maid, a dark girl with big eyes. She was folding laundry. She had the waist of Maria Theresa's, his daughter's, jeans under her chin and her arms were extended, she was smoothing, pulling. She froze, watching him. The madman, with his gun drawn, his eyes scoured the laundry room. He darted into

the maids' room, their bathroom, which was a toilet, a faucet, a
bucket, and a drain, as if they would choose to make love there,
Isabel and Doro—and then he stopped, and then it first occurred to
him that they were not in the house and he looked up and saw
Loling look at him, her eyes widened in disbelief, in fear, and then,
that child, skinny and dark, she looked away. There it was indelibly,
Loling, the *servant*, looking away so as not to embarrass him.

He flopped into the chair in the entrance-way next to the phone,
humiliated. And then it had nothing to do with the vision of his
wife fucking Doro. It had to do with the horrible knowledge that it
was her home, not his. Her family, her people who owned marble,
Chinese and Spanish antiques, caged attack dogs. The various
phone lines for convenience, the gold owl figurines from Burma.
Brass, ivory, designers who selected for you. It was she who owned
the very way the breeze carried through the house, a brilliance of
architecture. The potted jades, and someone trained to care for
them.

He knew her family did not want them to marry. But she was
stubborn, and they relinquished. They met in college. He lacked
discipline so they determined on the military where it took *favors
meant for her* even to make him a colonel. Doro and all the other old
friends were generals now.

The women had brought Bobby into the clique. His clothes
were nothing like theirs. He had not traveled. He invited nobody to
his home to meet his parents, but the women brought him in, he
was so charming, and the men, their brothers and boyfriends, they
had to accept him. He *had* been invited to the parties, Bobby De Los
Santos, the Handsome.

They even gave him begrudging respect because women adored
him. They worried about their own wives. But this was not why he
was not promoted further along. He was simply lazy, unauthoritative.

He had heard it, a circle, a conversation cluster at a gathering,
one of Isabel's girlfriends, a circle of men and women. He had been

returning from the restroom and he heard a woman's voice say "The Handsome" and a man's voice say "The Wife." And then men and women laughed.

He had been bought and cared for like a woman.

It was this. And he had—there was no restraining it—a profound urge to do the undoable.

He sat there with the phone, his finger on the reset button for a full thirty seconds, and then he called up his mistress, one of them, Heidi Hong, and told her the house was empty and to come as quickly as possible.

She was a nightclub manager, Heidi, and she was honored to be touched by the elite. She was terribly young and sexy.

Of course, Isabel and Doro arrived first. Of course, it was completely innocent. Hello Handsome, she said to Bobby, which only fueled his anger more. Doro will have dinner with us, she said, turning with her supposed elegance. She paused to gaze at Bobby who was so rooted to his seat, whose lips were trembling, and then, that bitch, she went on about her business with the slightest suggestion of a shrug.

Doro made a gesture, Doro stepped forward offering his hand with that big smile, as if to compensate for jealousy, but Bobby was heavy in his chair, like a drunk. Isabel went into the kitchen with directions for the cook, and Doro made himself at home, sat across the room, gazed about, attempted small talk. Bobby only sat still with his groping senile lips.

There was still time, he could have waited outside for Heidi's car and asked her to leave. This would have caused problems of smaller magnitudes, worthy of arguments, not life-changing. He could have whispered to a servant.

But he sat, rooted. Heidi rang the bell. He could have let Loling get the door, but he himself answered it. He could have gotten rid of her before Isabel returned from the kitchen. He did not. He allowed her to stand there and talk.

Doro stared in disbelief from his seat.

Isabel returned from the kitchen rubbing her hands together with activity, with her god damn *mission*. Her eternal list of things to be done. Heidi's body language was unmistakable. Isabel froze and her busy hands fell away, meant nothing.

And then a horrible expression passed over her face—peace. As if this were what she expected all along and as if it were a relief.

Three years later, Bobby stood, at the height of the rainy season, watching the water come down in sheets. It made mud of the yard, but it brought a clean smell. His arms were slung through the bars of his cell. This was unnecessary, really, this stance of such containment. Arms through the bars—as if that were the farthest he could reach into the world—yet the door was open and he could wander anywhere within the compound. He could pick up his umbrella and visit General Adelo across the way, or make his way to the kitchen and boil up some bananas. He could do any of this any time of day or night. The cells were never locked. This was minimum security. It was the old college buddies who had them incarcerated, really, and even a coup attempt is forgivable to Filipinos, a very forgiving people. Forgiving and fiercely loyal. The ties of having shared social circles, cliques, teams and dances and study groups in college—those ties were stronger than the workings of politics. The coup attempt, it was like having lost a soccer match. A touch of resentment for the time being, yes, but this too shall pass.

Oh, but that is, of course, an understatement. I mean only to emphasize that this might not be what is typically expected of prison. I do not mean Bobby was not deathly depressed. That he, and some of the others involved, did not lick out the mouths of insanity deep in the wee hours of darkness, in their cells, the insuf-ferable heat—even with fans, the electricity went out sometimes and they didn't have generators here like they had had in their homes. And Bobby, we might say he was worse off than the others, because, of the group, he was the outsider. He was not born to the elite and he had flirted with (but there was no proof) their wives. So when they needed a scapegoat, there he was. They ganged up on him at darts, didn't offer him the desserts their families brought, didn't share their video tapes. Just two days ago, Pauli Rosario, General Pauli Rosario (they were all generals, he was the only lesser officer fool enough to take part) had said Bobby could not borrow his work-out gloves because Cesar would be using them. And then Cesar sat in front of his cell all day long in a folding chair, playing cards and then reading.

Bobby had nightmares. He felt fundamentally unlovable. He was waiting for his wife with his arms slung through the bars of his cell. He reached just a bit farther than the awning and relished the sen-sation of the driving rain on the tips of his fingers. On the other side of the yard, through the blur of the water, he could make out that Adelo had a visitor—his wife, if she had changed her hair, and that the visitor was giving Adelo a hand massage. Bobby imagined the sensation and grew aroused. He longed for his wife. He counted on that tiny part of her which felt guilt.

His mind had been through many phases since he had been incarcerated, eighteen months now. He recognized now, that as long as he was imprisoned, his thinking would center around one idea for two or three weeks at a time. Center is not strong enough a word: cling madly, cling madly to a single idea and then suddenly it would be replaced. Now it was his cruel, cruel wife. How she was his only hope in the world and he had no choice but to accept every one of her whims.

A recent idea was hypoglycemia. He had read an article in a

magazine about its symptoms and discovered that he suffered all of them. That the hypoglycemic, when deprived of food for even a few hours, suffers a deterioration in higher cognitive ability, insomnia, the shakes. He lay awake at night feeling attacks coming on, stealing to the kitchen for snacks, and discovering that he had never eaten enough, went back for more snacks. He worked out twice as hard as any one else to compensate. He already had a naturally muscular body which needed no sculpting, but he had fear of losing it.

Then suddenly, he heard news from his cousins and the preoccupation with his blood sugar fell away. He could think of nothing but exacting revenge on the man who wronged his favorite little niece. The daughter of his favorite cousin, actually. The girl was only nineteen, and she was determined and studious. It was expected that she, like Bobby, would pull the family up, on another side, from another corner. She was one of the best students of her class, an orator, an organizer, and she could go into politics or run a business.

She was not pregnant, but she had been devastated. She had become a shell of her former self. Her grades plummeted. She refused to go out.

Bobby, for some time, spent his days fantasizing about *humiliating* the young man who had done this to her. At first his fantasies were intensely violent. Then they were simply words he could whisper in passing at a public gathering so the child (for he was only twenty, that boy) would live in fear. *Rodent. Insect. Pussy.* He had a rather complex idea about showing up at a disco with the young man's new girlfriend. The girl would, of course, look at Bobby with an adoration the young man had never experienced.

For some time, the colonel made plans for an acting career after his release. He even practiced posing in his mirror for publicity shots, and then wrote up a very convincing letter which could be sent to known directors. No, he had no training, but he had lived life the way few did, knew emotion more intensely. Thank god, he abandoned the letter before embarrassing himself. Now, Bobby could think of nothing but his wife.

She had left him matter-of-factly. She packed quickly, sent the servants home to the provinces and went off to Hawaii to live with her brother. She took their daughter. It was then that their daughter, Maria Theresa, developed that thick quality. She always looked as if she had just been woken from a deep, much-needed sleep. Yes, just before they left, Maria Theresa, her eyes were always puffy, not as if she had been crying, but as if she were *now finally* able to sleep. That expression never left her, that quiet staring heaviness. Isabel said she had had a suitor in Hawaii. He was shy and serious as well. It had developed painfully slowly.

They were gone not quite two years and Maria Theresa developed an American accent. Bobby felt she did it so that he would never forget they had left.

At some point, he realized that only the greatest of catastrophes would bring them back. Something had to take place where he was suffering more than she. At first he was convinced this would be a disease. Either blindness or cancer. His eyesight suddenly deteriorated. He saw white spots all day, almost completely clouded on the right. He would sit on the verandah at nightfall, smoking and making note of the changes. He could actually sense the minute changes in the way, it is said, a baby's growth is perceptible during the first year of life. Yes, now, the white splash which blocks my view of the fence, it is swelling, yes, wider now.

Then the coup presented itself. Are you with us or not? If they were victorious, he would be a hero. He would be a much larger man within the new government—and if they were defeated…

Isabel arrived that day, in a moment when the rain was waning. The generals stood in the doors of their cells and waved as she passed. She had a basket with her, filled with eggs, bananas, rice, Cheerios, and a new shower curtain. She said that Maria Theresa was not feeling well.

She crossed her legs and wiggled her foot. Bobby sat across from her, leaned forward onto his knees and clasped his hands.

"Well," he said.

"Yes," she said, and she poised her mouth as if to exhale smoke but she did not smoke.

"And so," Bobby said.

"Yes, and so…" said Isabel.

Bobby unclasped his hands, reclasped them and nodded slowly. Isabel, slightly and quickly, licked the corner of her mouth. Bobby had a question to ask of her. There was news he expected, but he could sense that she was feeling irritable, confrontational, and wanted to soften her. He felt desperate to soften her.

Her eyes were wide and black and staring fixedly unto his.

"My back," he said reaching around himself to indicate, wincing. She did not answer, as if she had not heard, so he repeated himself. "My back. You know what it is? Yesterday, I stepped…I thought I was stepping into the yard, and I stepped onto a stone. And the cushions, you know, the cushions between the links of the spine…"

Isabel shifted.

"You know, the soft part between the ones. It is as if I had no more. The links of my spine…" He slapped his hands loudly, precisely and dramatically, one against the other. "My muscles are deteriorating. What pain I felt. It was shocking. The sensation was, no, it was jarring."

It was not the story which constituted his plea, but his panting and grimacing. Isabel relented slightly by showing discomfort, by rolling her eyes a bit, looking away rather than staring stonily. He knew it was the time to beg of her. "Won't you, Isabel, won't you sleep here tonight?"

Their conjugal visits were unlimited, but Isabel seldom chose to exercise them. He faced her with his unabashed anguish. She looked away.

He did not sleep. Isabel rolled into him unknowingly, and though his arm began to tingle, he did not move lest he wake her.

Yes, and there had been thirty other seconds. They asked: Are you with us? And before he said *and if I fail she will come home*, he said *If we prevail...*

Smoke through the fingers, that flash in the periphery, his Glory Dragon.

DELICIOUS

NO ONE ever told Rebecca to be quiet in church. She fidgets when she's bored. She blows her bangs up off her face and scowls. She slaps her thighs and crosses her arms. She's a grown woman. In restaurants, she balances ashtrays on her head. Not to show off, but in the midst of conversation, the immediate answer to what to do with her hands, the time. She talks very very loudly. Sometimes she yells for no apparent reason, or she notices that the bottom ridge of the wine carafe is slightly wider than the top of her glass, like they were meant to fit together, like South America might float into the nest of Africa. She places the carafe on top of the glass—clink, clink, clink. If you are a polite person, a person who says please and thank you and sorry to trouble you, you cringe. If you are a polite person who does not know her, you probably very much dislike her. If you are a friend who loves her, you walk behind, crouching with your arms spread, catching things, bridging the distance, between Rebecca, whom you love, and the rest of the world. Shhhh-ing and explaining in glances to the waiter that you are not a party to this obliviousness.

Rebecca has a strong jaw, wild brown hair, and a long long neck. If you were falling out of love with her, the long neck would be the first thing to become absurd, but before that, it remains her most compelling feature.

Rebecca looks great with her hair tied back, bent and looking at her up-curled toes. The neck long enough to arch. When she stands, she lifts up up up on her body, a dancer about to turn. Her point of balance differs from the rest of ours.

She wears fake fur and has blunt manly fingers.

Now Rhonda, she's the croucher. She adores Rebecca and tries to calm her in unnoticed ways. When Rebecca starts yelling, Rhonda lowers her own voice and leans in, so that her friend might instinctively follow. Sometimes this works. Rhonda is always laying her fingers on Rebecca's forearm like the calming wife: in the theater when the lights go down, and Rebecca is still talking; in moments of confrontation Rhonda would rather were abandoned, when it's long past time to leave.

Rhonda, she is quite the opposite. She would never try to get free drinks from the bartender or ask a cab driver to stop in two places. After six years with the same hair stylist, Rhonda went in on a day he was sick, and a short shrill woman took his place. She never went back for fear of having to choose between them and insulting someone. She rarely enters clothing stores because all it takes is one "May I help you?" to obligate her to major purchases. She orders food when she's not hungry because she's sure that's what the waiter wants. She would never send anything back, no matter how raw the meat or rancid the vegetables. She says thank *you* after favors she herself performs and sorry when other people bump into her. She donates to charities over the phone.

Rhonda would follow Rebecca to the ends of the earth, cringing, with fingers on forearm.

Like most best-girlfriend groupings, they look something alike—the wild brown hair, the womanly build. But Rhonda is a bit shorter and distinctively bowlegged. Her neck is nothing like another limb. She's the thicker of the two, broad-hipped, with the pointy little chin of a slimmer girl.

They first met when Rhonda was just getting over her boy-friend. Her depression no longer carried his name, but was evolving into a vague and dull ache. His name only hung in the periphery. She was learning that simple things were not as tragic as they origi-nally seemed. She bought groceries and did her laundry more often, so that it wouldn't be too heavy for one person going up the stairs. So what if her sheets weren't folded as neatly? She took the books out from where they propped up her futon and fixed it, using a ham-mer for wedging and electrical tape for where the wood had chipped away. She felt very clever about that. She found these little rubber things in the hardware store that could be used, instead of a drill, to place screws. She gave her spare keys to a friend up the street, some-one more organized than Rebecca.

When Rhonda met Rebecca, she had just begun to laugh with-out making note of its falseness. Rebecca was very much associated with the seeds of Rhonda's joy.

Rhonda did not have a nickname for twenty-eight years, and then in her first six months as Rebecca's friend, she took on four. This was one place where Rebecca's attention was exacting, where she made mental notes, things to call Rhonda. She liked to make people laugh. There was "Ramda," because that is how it was mis-heard by the cab driver from Bangladesh, who said it meant, in his language "one sharp knife, okay?" "One Sharp Knife" was the sec-ond name. "Miss Thing" is what a lot of young people were calling each other at this time, and "Euthanasia" was an extensive joke played on another foreign cab driver, perpetrated entirely, of course, by Rebecca, while Rhonda pleaded for cessation with her eyes.

Rhonda gave names back but forgot to make them stick. She'd say it once or twice and either forget, or not consider them good

enough and try something new the next time. She considered "One
Sharp Knife" her own tribal Indian name, so she gave Rebecca
"Laughs Like Thunder" and then "Giblets" because Rebecca ate as
fast as one of those dogs they starve for TV commercials. In the
end, she called her Rebb, as Becky was too commonplace to suit
her.

Rebb—and of course it would be spelled with two *b*'s.

Rebb had a thing for cab drivers and she said she wanted to try
them in all flavors. She would slide in front and ask them where
they were from. The drivers would generally shift in their seats and
grow conscious of their wads of money. Rebecca sat sideways, staring. Rhonda scootched down low in the back seat so she wouldn't
have to watch the man's discomfort, the weirdness. Discomfort wasn't
always the case. Rebecca introduced them: this is Rhonda and I'm
Rebecca, Ramda and Rebecca, Euthanasia and Rebb. Rebecca would
put an elbow on the dashboard and one over the back of the seat.
She'd recite the few words she had learned in Hindi or Haitian
Creole or Spanish. There was an Egyptian named Raga, who had
only been in the city two months. This was a gypsy cab and his
English was poor and they had trouble getting where they were
going and the whole time Rebecca sat on her heels with her knees
toward him, as if he were the altar or the sand castle. She sat facing
him, her chest heaving and shaking with each bump in the road, her
head wobbling on that long and slender neck. He had amazing
hazel eyes and Rebecca asked him to come back later and then she
took him home. This made Rhonda so nervous that she cried.

Rhonda, who of course had been a wallflower, was forced to
start dancing in clubs. They would go to places where the median
age was nine years less than their own, and if Rhonda didn't keep
up, winding through the crowds, Rebecca would simply ditch her.
One night Rhonda said, "That's okay, Rebb, you go ahead," and
watched her friend shimmy in through the dance-floor. She stood

next to a speaker, sipping her white wine, anticipating the next day's earache. She turned down a grinning young man, horrified at his youth, at the thought that anything she'd do might be illegal. Rebecca did not come back. It might have been her on stage, where crowds of girls squeezed and bumped over the territory of the platform. It might have been Rebecca's red-sleeved arm rising and falling in rhythm, straight up and then dropping, noodle-like, as if all of her muscle had disappeared. Rhonda waited until the place closed, the lights went on, and then she went home alone, shaking with the pound of the bass.

After that, she danced. She held on to Rebecca's elbow and went where she went and found that it was usually dense enough with bodies to eat up her self-consciousness. One night, she arrived on the platform with dozens of much younger girls. They danced with their elbows out, so that if you got too close you'd hit that extended bone. Rebecca responded by dancing with her nails out. Rhonda had had enough to drink that night, so it was okay.

Rhonda did change, of course. She wanted to. She put on lipstick. Rebecca introduced her to push-up bras. Rhonda's laugh became throatier, her blushes less frequent. One night, after a rock 'n' roll show, Ramda had a thing with the twenty-year-old drummer. His teeth were small and wide apart, floating white chicklets. His smile was all gums. This is most of what she remembers. She left while he slept, regretting it only for a few days.

No matter what happened, Rebecca was always wilder. If Rhonda's skirt was short, Rebecca's was transparent. If Rhonda went home with the drummer, Rebecca had her way with the rhythm guitar in the restroom of the bar. Rhonda always had plenty of room to be the good girl.

It wasn't a complete tyranny of Rebecca's impulse. There was an argument or two. Rhonda lent Rebecca her bathing suit and didn't hear about it for a few weeks.

"Hey, um, do you still have my bathing suit?"

"Yeah, Ram. Listen, I had my period in it, pretty bad. Do you want me to buy you a new one?"

"Yes." It was the harshest word Rhonda had yet had for Rebecca, and it sounded as impotent as it was.

There was a night during the early sweet freshness of spring when Rhonda started dancing with a guy who was only a few years younger. He wore overalls and was really quite attractive. However, at one moment, she took a break and spoke to Rebecca and told her that he was too cheesy and pretty for her taste. Too much gel, and his hairline grew too far over his ears.

She kept dancing with him. She started making out with him. He had this way of kissing which was to go at it very gently for a while and then to grab and squeeze her suddenly and dramatically. Rhonda enjoyed this very much. They ended up on a couch in a back corner of the club, she on his lap, hands everywhere. When the lights went up, she said she had to go and he asked if she remembered his name. "Carl," she said, but it was Kevin. Rhonda laughed. "Do you remember mine?" she asked. She had told him but he hadn't the slightest idea. She thought this was funny and told him it was nice and too perfect and that now it was time for her to go home. He asked for her number and she refused, laughing. She wouldn't even tell him her name.

She told Rebecca in the cab on the way home, and Rebecca leaned back over the front seat and called her "Miss Thing" and slapped her five. Rhonda was hungry when she got home and ate an enormous bowl of Corn Chex with bananas on top, sitting on her bed in her pj's. She giggled to herself and thought of the young man, of how the evening was a fond moment she would always have. Her eyes welled up with tenderness, her love for Rebecca, the fun. She felt very very happy. She felt it couldn't get better from here. She felt her life coming into its own.

She felt she had had her adventures and wouldn't need them so much any more. She knew what she wanted out of life, a few of the possibilities condensing and floating to the top. She was, in this moment, at peace.

Rhonda spent less and less time with Rebecca. Although this made her love her all the more, it was in a different way. Rhonda knew that Rebecca had given her some of her most delicious memories. On a good, still day of reflection, the things a mind offers up as gifts, a little chuckle.

Rhonda commenced some of her own career-related projects. Had nice dinners with nice people, dated here and there.

Hours with Rebecca were passed in a state of nostalgia, with a soft grin at that year. Some things stayed with Rhonda. She maintained the ability to introduce herself. She liked to paint her face on the weekends.

But when Rhonda went to the clubs, she let Rebb leave her on the edge of the dance floor. This was actually a relief.

Of course, there would be depression to Rebecca's mania. There would be the night in the midst of Rhonda's wildest year, a time after she stopped sniffling at Rebb's pick-ups, but before she herself owned any flirtations.

The first time, Rebecca buzzes Rhonda's buzzer in the wee hours of the morning. The initial jolt, Rhonda incorporates into her dream. The second wakes her. On the third, she sits, quick and upright, eyes rolled off, ears tuned for listening. On the fourth and fifth and sixth, she tightens and hopes for the end.

She answers.

"It's me." Rhonda buzzes Rebecca in, wondering if she can shake off sleep enough for whatever adventure her partner in crime has come to drag her to.

Rebecca hobbles in the doorway, her fake black fur sliding off her shoulders, a jug of apple juice hooked over her finger. She is not drunk. She is not herself.

"Oh, hi. I know you were sleeping. I'm sorry." This is the first of Rebecca's tentativeness. Instead of maintaining her usual obliviousness, she seems to be clutching at Rhonda's reactions. Rhonda's surprise makes her strained smile twitch, her voice dip. "You can go back to sleep. I'll just sit." She clacks into the bedroom and parks on the edge of Rhonda's bed.

"Are you okay? Why are you here?" Rhonda is dumbfounded, hovering.

"I'll just drink my apple juice. You go back to sleep." Rebecca unscrews her jug and swigs, half of it running down her chin. "I spilled it. I'm sorry." Rebecca checks Rhonda's face and sees that her eyebrows are scrunched, mouth slightly open. Rebecca shudders. "Oh, of course you can't sleep if I sit here."

Rebecca clacks into the bathroom and sits on the edge of the tub. Rhonda turns to watch her. Rhonda follows and stares from the open door.

"I'll just sit here and drink my apple juice." This time she doesn't spill until she removes the jug from her mouth and she douses half her coat.

Then Rebecca covers her ears with her elbows straight out, like she's trying to squash the shape of her head. She screams without sound, with her mouth stretching open across her teeth, like a snake, like her pointy tongue should leap and retract. She gasps. And then she screams audibly. She sobs uncontrollably, like a baby tiring itself for sleep, but Rebecca never tires. Like a humiliation beyond comprehension. Like a grown woman should never cry. She moans so that the neighbors knock on the walls.

Nothing Rhonda does can quiet her. Not pressing face to bosom, not squeezing her hand. Rebecca will not pause her howling to answer why. Eventually, Rhonda leads her to the bed and tucks her in, where the bellowing continues. At least it doesn't echo so much into the next apartments. When Rhonda shuts the door to pace in the living room and think, the sound is slightly muffled.

She considers calling the hospital, the cops, but fears that tomorrow, when this has to be over, Rebecca would never forgive her.

She calls the girlfriend up the street who has her spare set of keys.

"Allison? I'm sorry. Yeah. I'm sorry. Does your roommate still have that Valium? I'll explain when I get there."

Rhonda trusts the consistency of Rebecca's crying to keep her for a quarter of an hour.

The Valium works, although it is a challenge to get the pills in her mouth, and even more to get the water in and the swallowing done. Rhonda tilts Rebecca's head back. She winds her fingers through Rebecca's hair and pulls. Rhonda grips solidly, pries Rebecca's chin down with the other hand, so that her friend's mouth hangs open to the sky. This is all ritual. No one can be forced to swallow.

There are second, third, and fourth times to this episode. Rhonda obtains a stash of Valium. Rebecca learns to take it voluntarily. The doses go up.

This is the other Rebecca. Rebb claims to have no recollections, although Rhonda suspects she's lying from embarrassment.

The fifth time is well into the content part of Rhonda's life. This comes on a night when Rhonda is worn out with her accomplishments of the last few days. When Rhonda has done so many things for the good of her future that her body is throbbing with weariness. A very satisfying fatigue. She has been too busy with life to get sleep. She is so tired that all she is doing is staring at the TV, working up the strength to ready herself for bed.

Next to her on the couch is a baked potato with cheddar cheese and broccoli, only a few bites taken out of it. Her stomach was rumbling, but it was a chore to chew, and besides, she had seen blue in the potato. A rotten little cloud that showed up after broccoli was picked away.

She is balled up on the couch with her coat over her backward for a blanket. She never got it to the closet. It is all she can do to keep her eyes open. She promises herself to get up at the next commercial.

She makes a mental list of what needs to be done. The radiator should be turned up, which means a clanging in the pipes for a few good hours, but she'll be so knocked out she won't notice. She needs to put the uneaten food in the kitchen and do all the regular stuff: brush her teeth, take off her shoes, etc. She must repeat a list to herself because she is tired enough to forget.

She considers the possibility that the potato wasn't rotten because she is seeing blue spots everywhere. Red spots, blue spots —she is blindingly weary. She takes a deep breath and forces herself up before she crashes right there.

She turns up the radiator, and the clanging and sputtering pipe in. She enters her bedroom to kick off her shoes, and then the buzzer.

And there is Rebecca, so pale and pasty that she looks like the dead skin under a band-aid. Rhonda's coat is still on backward, arms through the sleeves, flapped open in back. One shoe is off.

Rebecca is already blubbering. Rhonda adds her to the mental list of things to do. Put Rebecca to bed. Hang up her coat. She lays Rebecca on her bed and goes to get the Valium and a glass of water. She brushes her teeth. She goes back to the bedroom and kicks off her final shoe but feels such a rush of exhaustion that she decides to get in bed fully dressed. She makes sure Rebecca takes the Valium, then huddles herself around her sobbing friend, and falls right out into a deep dense sleep.

If it had only been Rebecca. If there had not been the clanging of the heater, the sputtering, iron knocks. Rhonda was dead to the world.

But there she is, only a few hours later, Rebecca stretched next to her on the bed wailing, with her eyes bugged out like a little man kicked them forward from the inside.

Rhonda wants sleep more than anything. Rhonda gets two more Valium and a glass of water and hands them to Rebecca, but Rebecca will not take them. Rhonda tries to open Rebecca's mouth, but the tantrum now includes rolling her head from side to side, twisting and yanking from right to left on that unreal neck. Twisting and yanking as random and incomprehensible as the striking of the radiator. If there had been a rhythm—to the radiator, to Rebecca's snotty screaming—Rhonda could still be asleep. Rhonda would have made a song of it in her dreams.

But Rebecca won't hold her head still for the Valium. So Rhonda gets on top of her, sits right on her stomach, and pins her arms with her knees. Rhonda's backward coat bunches between them on Rebecca's chest. Rebecca kicks, but her voice is quieted because Rhonda has a hand over her mouth. Rhonda grabs Rebecca by the hair and pries open her jaw, which takes all of her strength, and pours water in and drops in the pill but Rebecca gurgles and spits it up. It lands in Rebecca's hair. Rhonda picks it up and tries again and Rebecca spits it up again.

And Rhonda's adrenaline has kicked in. It is not sleep that she wants more than anything. What she wants more than anything is to beat the shit out of Rebecca.

Rhonda was an athlete in high school, and it has been a very long time since she felt that anticipation and lift, that strength surging before the event. That strength worked for, longed for, and given from the most surprising places, and this moment is just like the moments before the events when she was twelve years younger. Her lungs are fuller than they've been in twelve years. Her senses as astute and willing. She takes Rebecca's head by the hair, like she would try to force the Valium once again, but this time, she smacks her.

SO MUCH

LIAN LIKES TO SIT with her misery on the front stoop. She wants to have witnesses. The neighbors might spy through their curtains, through the slats of their blinds. The eyes of passers-by linger ever so slightly on her huddled form. They think they're not staring, but Lian knows from the way they look away that they have made note of her quiet and noble suffering.

Languid in her sadness, Lian's eyes run slightly. She sniffles. She is fourteen, and her boyfriend has left her, or quit her, rather, because it's not like a boy of fifteen has someplace to go. Now she'll have to face him at school. This is very humiliating, but Lian bears it. She sets her jaw and stares out over the street.

Lian's misery has a name. It is "I was so much in love."

Lian's mother, Ina, does not appreciate Lian's dramatics on the stoop. Lian likes to be there waiting when her mother gets home, when the sun goes orange through the buildings. This little show is worth the price of Ina's anger. Lian must have the world know how it is between them. Sometimes Ina curses loudly and tells the girl to get inside and sometimes Ina only speaks with her rattling keys. She pretends Lian is not there, but her keys rattle more than keys really rattle.

A few times, Lian was smoking, and in these cases Ina would grab the cigarette and grind it with her heel. This is on her silent days. On her yelling and cursing days, Ina might bend to a breath from her daughter's face. Then Ina would flick the cigarette half way across the street. Ina has flicked cigarettes in her life and knows how to flick it that far. And then, that slight breath away, Ina would say, *get inside*, and Lian would feel the soft spray of her mother's saliva.

Ina is tired when she gets home from work. Ina has spent the whole day longing for this moment, this getting in the door and setting down her things, and there is Lian moping and trying to make her mother look bad. Lian is such a child, and Ina was not like that when she was fourteen. This is both a good and bad thing.

Oh, but today, Ina is an expert. Today Ina, hungry for the stuffed chair upstairs, bids her daughter good evening, turns her key deftly, and climbs. Ina climbs four flights, past the man who scolds his dog all day, past the woman who drinks beer in the morning, to Ina's own rooms. She does not turn on the light. She drops her bag by the door and falls into the stuffed chair with her jacket still on. Her hips are on the edge of the seat, her neck to its back.

Lian, frustrated on the stoop, cuts her eyes at the street. She slits the whites and black to half. She yanks at her own ponytail. Lian is a thin, brown girl. Her frame is delicate. Her movements are large and precise. Her boyfriends quit her because of her hands. This boyfriend and the last. Lian cannot control her hands, her slim and tapered fingers. When she is angry, or even just startled, her hands fly, backhand, forehand. She doesn't slap hard, but still, there is such a thing as pride. The first, he hit her back twice. This last one didn't bother. He was a sweet boy. His laugh went through three stages. A wheeze and a snort and a bellow.

When Ina was a girl, she was so much in love, like Lian is now. Ina was crazy for love. She loved him so much. She watched his shoulder blades through his shirt, through skin. He moved his arms and his shoulder blades moved. The surface of water. So much muscle and tautness. She lay her cheek between them and listened to his blood.

He was a soldier and he died. In this place where Ina raises her daughter, a girl is allowed many boyfriends. This was Lian's second already; next month she can have a new one. This is what they do.

There are days when Ina's apartment feels very unclean, when every particle of dust makes itself known. Ina's eyes linger on nail holes, the places paint has chipped. Grey streaks run over tiles, curl up in the corners. She absorbs grey in her heavy, after-work breathing.

Lian comes bounding up the stairs. It is amazing that such a slight girl can make so much noise with her steps, as if she jumps and then lands, jumps and then lands. Lian knocks. Ina does not stir. Lian waits. She presses her ear to the door, knows her mother is in the stuffed chair. "*Maaaaa,*" Lian calls, not all too kindly, curling her lip. "*Maaaaa.*" She knocks again before she finds it unlocked.

Lian stomps past her mother into the bedroom. Slams that door. He had said she was very pretty. He had tilted her face with one finger, just to look. He had looked closely. Lian can make such ugliness in her life. Why must she make such ugliness? He was drinking Seven-Up from a bottle and her hand flew to the back of his head. He knocked his teeth on the glass—you could hear it. Nothing broke. They were lucky. He had said something about another girl. It might have been nothing. This was all about nothing about another girl. Lian lights a cigarette; her long pink thumbnail twitches at the filter.

The light makes an L out of the bedroom, and the smoke comes with it. Ina shifts. She listens to her daughter throw things and growl—a pillow, a shoe, nothing breakable. Ina is waiting for her own boredom to grow stronger than her weariness. This is the way she knows her rest is over, when she can no longer bear to sit still. Usually, she has that kind of energy. Today, she could sit forever. She watches the smoke and the dust and the angles of light.

Lian throws open the door, stands in shadow, her arms on either side of the frame. "Why you sit there in the dark like that, Ma?" she implores. "You just *sit* there." Ina turns her head to look but does not answer. Lian slams the door.

Lian does not understand that in no way is this darkness. There are always tiny, glowing things. The street lamps spread through the heaviest curtains; the hall light seeps under the door. In this darkness that is not darkness, you can see things. The outline of Lian's limbs moves with her sounds. The wind—the apartment's second great noisemaker after Lian—you can see how it carries the curtains, knocks and pulls them against the window grates. Sometimes, Lian watches TV with the sound off after Ina wants to sleep. Ina sleeps in the living room. The girl sits in the stuffed chair as her mother dozes, Ina's face flashing blue and orange with the screen.

Where Ina comes from, where Lian was born but does not remember, there were nights of darkness. Not always, but when the moon slivered to nothing and they were left with black and sound.

There is no place in the world that is silent. On the darkest, most windless days there are insects and breath. In this place where Ina raises her daughter, there are pipes and voices, sirens, honking, humming things—the refrigerator, planes overhead, a neighbor's radio two flights down.

Where Ina comes from, on the quietest, most windless, breath and insect days, they would, sometimes under the weak light of the moon, sometimes in the black, they would hear the slowest, most careful footsteps. Slow careful footsteps, but still, they would hear, unless they were asleep, the footsteps, if they were on the path or through the fields. They could tell if the footsteps crunched pebbles or rustled through the fields. Unless they were asleep, and they slept so lightly in those days. The worst were the days full of rain, when there were too many sounds for knowing.

There are things to watch in this apartment, in Lian's supposed darkness. There is the square of pale brightness falling over the back of the TV, the way the brightness sways. There is the dust and Lian's smoke. The glow of metal things, the knob of the TV, the legs of its stand.

Lian is moaning.

Ina throws a hand to her own forehead, calls through the closed bedroom door, "Daughter, your mother is weary today, won't you make the dinner?" This is Ina's concession. This is the best she can do. She doesn't have to ask twice; Lian comes banging out, her ponytail leaping, her nose and eyes red. She wears a blue flannel shirt that hangs to her knees, nothing on her legs and big white sweat socks, like she's ready for bed.

Lian turns on the kitchen light. Ina's eyes wince. Lian makes everything hit something: the cabinet door hits the one next to it, the pot hits the burner, the lid hits the pot. Every separate grain of rice falls with resonance. The knife lands with a thud to the chicken, the carrots.

Ina stretches, removes her jacket. She turns on the TV and sits back down. The volume is off from Lian's watching the night before. Ina leaves it that way. "Won't you get your mother some tea while she waits?"

Lian rattles a cup of tea out to her mother. She stands over Ina, her hands on her blue flannel hips. Ina takes a hot mouthful too quickly, pats at her throat to soothe.

"In case that you might care, Eddie broke up with me." Ina meets her daughter's eyes to let her know that she has heard.

Ina turns back to the TV. She smothers an impulse to curse her daughter. It is not love when he does not love you back.

After a time, Lian shoves her mother a plate and stomps with her own into the bedroom. There is the sound of wailing inter-rupted by chewing.

The things they fight about are silly. Lian is a disrespectful daughter. That is how they are, these children, and Ina, at some point, grew too tired to raise a hand to her.

Yesterday, Ina spent the whole work day thinking of her daugh-ter, of how joyfully fat Lian was the year they first came. Ina dug her lips into Lian—cheeks and belly and butt—the softness, the flesh. Ina spent the day reflecting on her fat child, and wanting to make peace with the young, thin woman. She bought her a gift. Chocolates in a box with a ribbon. Ina was choked up all day with the idea. She would give the box to her daughter and it would be known that Ina wanted Lian to have pleasure in her life.

"I don't like this kind, Ma," Lian said, and Ina, who could no longer raise her hand, felt her will for anger slip.

Lian burns candles in her room. This is a hobby of hers. She drips blue wax on the back of her hand, scrapes it, and rolls it into balls. She loves that warmth that does not burn. She smokes and smokes and smokes, and Ina says nothing. Eddie had taken her face by the chin, just looking.

She made him sick with love. She is obese and smothering with love. She drops cigarette butts in half a bottle of Ginger Ale. She watches the brown streaks curl up through the goldish fluid. She's like the taste you'd get if you drank it.

For a moment, Lian's loss is too terrible to be real so she goes for the telephone, which is opposite her mother and the stuffed chair. She calls and is told Eddie is not home.

Ina's greatest regret is the relief it brought. In the first disbelieving moments, she took it as a waiver. She took the tragedy for herself, thought of the redemption it could bring. She had fallen out of favor with the family. She had been running with a boy. This had been a very bad thing, but it was nothing in comparison to this later tragedy. Ina had had trouble sleeping, knowing her parents were shamed by her, knowing her parents would watch her every move, keep her from the boy. Her father had beaten her. She had had trouble sleeping, so she was the one awake and she heard when they came rustling through the field.

They came, and it was her sister they took, and Ina knew her own wrongdoing was erased. Her petty offenses were forgiven. They came for her sister and this was Ina's first thought. Her second thought, was no, please, but nothing she thought or felt afterwards would erase the fact that she had taken this suffering for her own ends.

By the time they came for Ina herself, it was just she and her mother. Ina had been dreaming of fat for four days. Before the fighting, in those vague and petty days, they had kept a can of fat for cooking. When they were done, they poured the leftover grease into a metal can and kept it for next time. When they poured it back out, it was solid and had a tube shape with ribs. For four days, Ina could do nothing but dream of fistfuls of lard, of dipping into that can-shape and licking her fingers.

So this is what Ina did. His breath smelled distinctly of fat. So she kissed him. He thought she was crazy, mocking him. He hit her with his closed hand. He held her face away by the hair. But she had had enough time to drink his fat. She wiped every trace in one swoop. She licked his gums and cheeks and tongue, and this gave her strength for two days.

And so Lian. Lian crying in her room that she loved him so much. Ina's dancing, gum-chewing, sobbing daughter.

Ina takes her in arm, at the same time admonishing herself for contributing to Lian's weakness. Lian hugs so tightly. Lian has been famished for hugs. Ina rocks her. Ina must teach Lian to love like a person labors. Next time, Ina will be stronger and teach Lian the tricks of life. Loving like a person labors, like when you work and are weary and work on, and the stomach pains come, thirst or exhaustion, the cramps, and you breathe a certain way, contract certain muscles to lessen it as much as possible. But at the same time you accept the pain and expect that it will pass. You have to believe that it will pass, fifteen minutes, an hour, two. In life, those you love will be gone, and even when you do love with such fierceness— because you will, everyone will love with such fierceness—you must breathe a certain way until it passes.

THE NEXT PLACE

ALMA was in the big house. She played in the front room doing things she was not supposed to do. She pushed open the wooden slats of the window and watched the sun divide into its raging angles. She watched dust float. She ran her fingers through it. Mother would be angry. It was too hot for this. It was so hot and wet you could swallow it. Alma put her face to the light and felt where one part grew moist.

There was a table in the front hall. If Alma were really brave, she could stand on the table and push the blades of the ceiling fan. They don't turn on their own. She might need a broom. Alma twists her chin up toward the fan. Her black hair sticks to her face. Her hands are on her hips.

She was playing. She was half in a dream. Not in so many words, not literally, but in essence, Alma says to herself, there is no other way to say this. *There are no other words. There was never any other way.*

They lived in the big house with all their cousins and aunts and uncles. Some of the uncles were gone. Tiyo Manuling was in the church yard with the Japanese for four days. When he came back, he walked as if he were obese, with his limbs spread away from the center. He said there was a sea of bats in the church. They cried when he left and when he came back. Auring—she's the youngest of Alma's aunts—she's been hardened and she yells at her sisters for crying.

They used to live in Manila. Alma used to go to school but the teacher stole her lunch. Alma has no father. Leling is her mother.

The soldiers chase the chickens in the yard. They bark. They carry bayonets. Leling yells about the children from the window, through the rattling shell lattice. The children need the chickens. Her voice is high pitched and wavering, but loud. They don't understand each other's languages, Leling and the Japanese, but when they yell back, she knows that she must stop.

Leling has three children. One is dark and one is light and the third is still a baby, so that it is too soon to tell. Their grandfather used to call the light one Banana Butt. That was his favorite joke. Come here, Banana Butt. Time for dinner, Banana Butt. Now four sisters and one brother live in the big house with their eleven collective children. Auring lives in the room with Leling and Leling's three because she has none of her own.

Leling's voice is high pitched and wavering, but loud.

Nobody sleeps. Leling feels herself falling falling, but whenever she truly nears she is yanked away.

They sell things one by one. Candlesticks, silver, Chinese porcelain. They sell all the glistening things. They dig things up from under the trees at night. They turn the damp earth. No one sleeps anyway. Auring, the boldest of the sisters, she trades with the black market. She's the one. Her husband is dead. We know this for a fact. Men come with bundles on their backs. One man had slippers.

They were made of wood and rubber tires and he wound them together with hemp, carried it all on his back. Auring showed him a candlestick and he came back with chickens at night.

There was never any other way. The teacher took her lunch. There is a table in the front hall. Alma puts her chin to it and stares directly at the white light between the window slats. Mother would be furious, but mother is somewhere else. Alma opens one eye then the other. She wants to see if the patterns your eye makes, if the purple clouds your eye makes are different with different eyes or with the length of time you stare.

Leling fell asleep with her arm to the net. It was only for so long, an instant of her nearing. She woke and the whole length along the back of her arm was raised and burning. Auring cared for Leling's children for a while.

Leling gets a message from a servant. He is really still a boy. He traveled all this way, out here to the province, to the boondocks. Leling feeds him and he eats voraciously. She fears for his eating so fast. He talks while he eats. Nothing is written down. He eats with his fingers.

He says the lady of the house, Leling's friend, sends word. From her house in Manila, from the second story window, you can see into what was once the university.

This is the richest, plushest land. We just reach out for fruit.

It takes much planning and many secrets. Many months ahead, it is said April 1st. And then Leling takes her girl, the dark one. It is them and two young men who they pay with rice. Alma's hair is wound in coils to the sides of her head. The car gasps and spits. Leling's mouth stays grimaced in a half-yawn. She winds her fingers around Alma's forearm. Alma's arm begins to tingle.

The bridge is out. They use planks. First Leling and Alma and one young man walk across and then the other takes the car.

Always the horrible stench. A face now carries this expression of breathing against the stench.

Alma meets her Auntie Isabel. She is a crouched, plotting woman. She rubs her hands together. They don't say much. She takes them upstairs and slides the window open.

"Stand here," Leling says, placing Alma in the window.

Isabel explains quickly. There is a house in the way, but if they look around, they can see a corner of what was the campus. There is barbed wire over the fence, steel ivy. They can see three tiny men. They have no shirts. They squat and dig and then stand, squat and dig and then stand. One man faces them. The men have no skin. They are the color of blood and the size of bones.

Isabel says here, look, and she comes with binoculars and she bends against the window pane. All that would show would be the top of her head and the binoculars against the edge.

"Okay. Okay." Leling says. "We'll just wait a moment first." She says it in English by mistake. Silver, cold trickles through Alma's veins, a sense of perversity.

You cannot imagine what you have not seen. You would never imagine it right. Alma's lower lip pulses. She looks to her mother. The men in the wire are the most angular people she's ever seen. And then concave between the angles. From here she can see that their bones suck as if inhaling fabric. This is a dream without screams.

They stand for a time, and then Leling bends with the binoculars to the window for a time, and then she hands them to Alma.

"He's the one facing us," she says, high pitched, wavering. Alma does not want to look but must. There is a man bent over a hole and he is staring at Alma with his horrible eyes. He is skinless, the color of blood, and his hair is as white as the sun and his eyelids are as thick, as swollen as fists, as if he has stuffed something up in there. He's hiding food or cloth or coins.

This must be the next part. There was never anything else. There will be no big house nor her mother. Alma, gathering gathering up in a way that she knows, she stays herself. She would hurl herself screaming. She would wind herself in a vice.

In the end they'll run from fire. The roads burn as fuses, impossible wet fuses, and yet. Wet land burning. Monsoons of fire. They'll take the raft. Their children don't scream. Senseless, dumb. These deaf mutes. Who are these children who don't scream?

THE GREAT ARTIST

IN THE SPRING of 1991, the world's greatest drummer made love to Andrea, a sweet, young footsoldier of New York's aspiring. By "made love" I do not mean "performed the sex act gracefully and with a certain tenderness." No, by the time the two of them actually consummated the affair, it was quite pathetic. Andrea was madly enraptured and the Great Artist was afraid of how she would latch herself on to him. (He had been through this before, girls who call all day, hurl themselves crying in public places, beg.) Yes, the moments of intimacy were flavored by his attempts at distance and her desperation. He hardly enjoyed it. He could see all that shit coming. And Andrea, she was swooning. On another planet all together. She was overwhelmed. Her eyes rolled back in her head. She could barely speak.

By "made love," I mean he made an overture, came to visit more than once, charmed and flattered her, dropped enough information to reveal his identity. (He had recently defected, and had not yet worked his way up through the ranks in New York. Only true afficionados with obscure record collections from his native land would know him.)

Andrea (who pronounced her name on-dray´-uh) was twenty

years old, such a pretty thing, from the Midwest. She had half a B.A. and had been in the City not much longer than he, eight months. She had come with some vague notion of being somebody and stood day after day, dressed in her black mini-skirt, in that quaint little restaurant on the Upper West Side where the Defector found her. Shift upon shift, she fetched and carried things, her legs buckling with weariness, waiting for that moment of glory to descend from the sky. *No, I'm not an actress,* she told those who cared to ask, although she was secretly waiting to be discovered.

O who could blame the Great Artist—who was used to the best dancers, the rebel daughters of politicians. He was new to this country. For a blind moment, he was lonely and forgot who he was. He was actually nervous the first few times he approached her, his voice shook. He said she had pretty hair. He said things that made her blush and look off.

Andrea, not being the most aggressive girl in the world, she only called three times after it was all over, only went to see him play once. He was cold and rude on the phone and formally polite when she came with three girlfriends to sit in the back of that smoky little jazz club. By then, he was well up the mountain and had taken up with a refined art dealer. He barely spoke to Andrea. Her girlfriends cursed him and consoled her. She could no longer deny it.

It took her, after one night with him, five months to accept that it was over. And then she thought about it every day for almost two years. It nearly drove Andrea over the edge, but she learned something essential to a girl with an impulse toward a greater life, any call to beyond, to glamour, for a girl too short to be a model and too shy to make herself an actress: she was goodlooking enough for men she considered important to pay attention to her. Andrea eventually discovered that she was not just pretty, but if dressed carefully, if in a good mood, she was stunning.

We join Andrea in the spring of 1995, four years, nearly to the day, after the Season of the Great Artist. She worked at a better restaurant by then, owned the wardrobe of an advancing professional. (Waiters in the right place in New York can make what lowlevel lawyers make.) And one thing the G.A. gave her, after all the tears and suffering—was that no one would ever be quite as good as him, no one she had been lucky enough to run across, anyway, and no one made her nervous.

Who could compete with the world's greatest drummer? Certainly not the assistant manager whom Andrea weaseled the best shifts out of for those last few months of summer, her twentythird year. She upset the rites of seniority and pissed everybody off, created so many enemies among the waitstaff, that she finally left for other employment. Not the supporting actor from that low-budget film. Not even the producer, that twenty-seven-year-old Boy Wonder of rap videos, the young Puerto Rican (she was inclined toward Latin men) who also did that Saturday afternoon positive energy show. He was ashamed of dating the most *gringa* of *gringas*, took her only to the most out of the way places or *home—to her place*—but spent lots of money on her nonetheless. No, the producer had little to no press about him. She, Andrea (born an *dree-a, as you would expect, and christened "Ondrayuh" upon arrival in New York by her own damn self) she couldn't regularly stop into a magazine store, open a magazine, and browse until she found an article about the Boy Wonder of rap. Cute, yes, promising, yes, but no provéd genius. No, that could only be done with the Great Artist.

Certainly, Raimundo, her date on this particular evening in the spring of 1995 was nothing to quiver over. By coincidence, he was a Latin drummer, as well. He was Portuguese and here to study with renowned teachers. It bothered Andrea that he found instructors necessary. Besides that, Ondrayuh found his outfit embarrassing, showed the influence of heavy metal: pointy boots, a studded belt. His hair was feathered. She had met him in a tapas bar, had over-heard him talking about being a musician and so preened in his gen-eral direction. She didn't expect to like him enough to even want to go out with him, only wanted to capture his attention, to make note of so much. But in the midst of conversation, he said that he knew Maria de Medeiros, the actress from *Pulp Fiction*, who played Anaïs Nin in *Henry and June*. (Andrea had thought she was French.) He said that the artistic community in Lisbon was very small, that she was a good friend of his, that she liked foosball, and then, well, Andrea thought he just might do for a while. She thought she would have a lover in Lisbon and she could go the upcoming summer.

And so there they were on the train, heading toward Andrea's friend's party in Brooklyn. It was a long wide car of the B with seats only along each wall. Across from them sat an old Russian woman with a resolutely dour expression, and next to her, a teenager in baseball cap who appeared to be her companion. The kid was pick-ing at a scab on his collarbone.

Raimundo did the talking. He was a talker. He told his life story. He said he had gone to a lot of different schools, that he went to a German school and later studied in French and was sent to Spain for a semester. He said he got kicked out of these places. This gave Andrea the opportunity to flatter him, oh, you're a fighter, huh? And relieved her as well, because she herself had dropped out. It also made her like him just a bit more, as he was so cultured.

She asked him what kind of music he played, and he said every-thing from jazz and bossa nova to rock and roll. She mentioned the American band from the Boston area, Extreme, who had had a big hit a few years previously. They all had Portuguese names, the chil-dren of immigrants. They had that metal aesthetic, yet their big hit was a ballad. Then came a moment where they watched the kid across pick at his scab and exchanged looks of disapproval. Andrea crossed her legs importantly and threw back her hair. She felt people in the car were looking at them. Certainly the kid with the skin problem was listening, squinting at the lanky European. Andrea knew the kid was running the MTV loop in his mind, trying to fig-ure out who Raimundo was. Andrea was a bit sad that Raimundo wasn't well known, but she allowed this feeling to pass, fall through her like a rush of embarrassment.

The old woman shifted her dour expression, lifted her mouth and resettled it as a lady smooths her skirt under her ass. The door opened between stops and the sound of sirens wafted through. Raimundo and Andrea looked at each other and smiled. Andrea described the town where she was from and Mundo, as he told her to call him, nodded.

As they walked to the party, Raimundo offered her his arm, and she slid her own through, but released it in the elevator to the apart-ment. She was still embarrassed by his outfit and didn't want her dear friend Tanya, Our Lady Tanya of Impeccable Taste (she worked for Donna Karan), to think Mundo was her *date* date.

The two friends greeted each other from some distance, their slim arms lifted, puckering and calling each other's names. Tanya was wearing a silk shirt through which her nipples were distinctly visible. She petted Andrea's hair and said she looked pretty. Tanya was beaming.

They were both unnatural blondes. It was Tanya who taught Andrea where to get the color that didn't look so ridiculous and how to maintain it. This was back in Andy's (that's what they called her back home) first few months in New York. Tanya was still at Parsons and they were waiting tables together.

"Let me show you the apartment," Tanya said, grabbing her friend's hand. Tanya and her roommate had been there just a couple of months and this was Andrea's first visit. They went on a tour of the two-bedroom place.

Mundo was left hovering in the doorway, his jacket slung over his arm. He grinned at a few people as they passed.

It was still early and there was a large contingent of marijuana smokers in the apartment, so that this was an unusually quiet party. Two girls sat Indian-style on the futon in the living room, staring straight ahead. Andrea knew one of them and said hello. The girl's eyes were thickened and her reactions were slow.

"You're so stoned," Andrea said.

"I'm sorry," said the girl she knew.

Tanya's bedroom was particularly intimidating as it was quite well-decorated. Over her bed was a small sunshaped mirror and everything else was minimal. It was very clean and her bed had white comforters. "Oh, Tanya, I wish I had your taste," Andrea said. And the two talked about having Tanya come over and redo Andrea's room.

By the time Andrea got back to Mundo, she felt a little guilty, so she turned to him, offered him her face. The contours were truly exquisite. She could see that he was moved. She let him gaze for a moment and then spoke.

"Tanya, this is Mundo," she said. And Tanya shook the musician's hand with what was clearly a look of tolerance. Mundo was very tall and skinny and his chin was weak. He was pale, downright sickly looking.

Not long after, coats arranged in the hall closet, crackers and cheese sampled, salmon spread, grapes; Raimundo and Andrea settled against the wall next to the refrigerator. They found vodka in the freezer and fixed themselves screwdrivers as the frost lifted in clouds into the room.

There were a handful of people in the kitchen, hovering over the food and warming up *sake* over the stove. Mundo and Andrea looked at each other and smiled. They lit cigarettes. Tanya drifted through, found a stash of brownies in the cupboard and quickly circled her guests offering the desserts. Andrea declined a brownie and Tanya moved on, not having noticed that she forgot to offer Mundo one. He was lifting bills from their magnetic holders on the fridge, looking at their undersides. Andrea looked at him apologetically.

"Don't worry about me," Mundo said, understanding her pity. "I can entertain myself." There was a touch of anger in what he said, and Andrea was flattered by it. She was also a bit relieved. If he was going to be angry, then she could retaliate and she allowed herself a good long look at an attractive young man standing straight across the long kitchen from them.

After some time, she made small talk with Mundo. This consisted of her wracking her brain for questions to ask him. She asked how he liked New York. She asked about other cities. Then she asked him about his family and he described his brother and his big house in Lisbon.

Andrea turned back to the handsome young man who was enacting something for a friend. He said, "Okay, okay, wait," (she could hear it from her corner) and came through the doorway of the kitchen in a walk that was not his own.

Andrea was getting madder at Mundo. Not only was he cramping her style, he never asked her about herself. She began to plot to get herself over near the other young man.

She excused herself toward the bathroom, set her drink on the fridge, and using all of her strength, did not let her eyes touch the object of her desire as she passed. She figured she had laid the groundwork in this way, would do it again on the way back, then check his response a few moments later. But when she returned, he was wrestling with his friend over the stove, yanking a bottle of *sake* this way and that, and could not experience her expressed disinterest.

Between Mundo and the refrigerator, where Andrea had just stood, there now appeared a towering curvaceous brunette with a distinctly tragic face. Her eyebrows lifted up toward the center in a

frozen moment of betrayal. She was passionately proposing something to Mundo, grabbing his forearm with one hand while the
other held a burning cigarette. This cigarette was perfectly vertical,
its glowing orange end up toward the ceiling, lodged between joints.
She was wearing a long, maroon, velveteen dress.

Andrea retrieved her drink from atop the freezer, and though
the glass was nearly full, she wanted it completely full and asked the
towering brunette to move so she could open the door and get some
ice.

"Andrea," Raimundo said, rolling the r, "this is Alexandra. She
is an architect." Andrea extended her hand.

"Nice to meet you," Alexandra said. She smiled. She asked
Andrea what she did and Andrea said she waited tables.

"Are you an actress?"

Everything this brunette said involved a great deal of facial
expression. This particular question was preceded by a poising of
the lips, not unlike a pucker.

"First of all," Andrea said, "not everyone who waits tables is an
actor."

Scouring her brains for a hot minute, Andrea could think of no
Second of All. She grew tired of Alexandra's expectant pose and
became distracted by the undersides of bills which clung by magnet
to the refrigerator.

It appeared that Alexandra had a friend in Jeffrey, a tousle-haired
young man in a blue turtleneck. He had just arrived and was also
very tall. "Jeffrey," Alexandra called, from across the room. They
kissed on both cheeks and embraced. She made introductions.
"This is Andrea. And this is Raimundo; he's a musician visiting
from Lisbon."

"Oh, a musician," said her friend in the blue turtleneck.

"Jeffrey here sang for a while." Alexandra's cigarette remained a
perfect geometric phenomenon.

"A singer!" Mundo widened his arms. He shook hands vigorously and touched Jeffrey on the elbow. "A singer. What type of singer?"

Jeffrey blushed. "Oh, nothing, a little new wave in the eighties, you know, kid stuff."

It was soon thereafter that, as if the marijuana contingent weren't mellow enough, Tanya's roommate put on the lingering trumpet CD, and it felled the volume of conversation for a moment.

"Ah," Mundo said, pointing toward the ceiling.

"Yes, it's beautiful," said the towering brunette, with her orange ember toward the heavens as well. When she said beautiful, her eyes squeezed shut.

They were quiet. Andrea smiled and offered her face to Jeffrey, who blinked unknowingly. She pondered his sexuality.

Mundo told the story of seeing a master trumpet player.

"You know, Mundo," said the tragic brunette, "yes, I am an artist of sorts, but…"

Now, although Andrea had begun not only to feel ambivalent toward, but to *dislike* Mundo, she considered it quite an offense that Alexandra felt she could simply place her huge body between Andrea and her date. So Andrea stepped between them. She felt actual contact between Alexandra's breast and her back. She slid next to Mundo, slipped her arm through his, so that Alexandra was forced to step back.

Mundo clasped Andrea's hand and looked her full in the face. Triumphant, Andrea allowed them to continue their conversation. Alexandra stepped around so that the four of them, Jeffrey included, made a close circle. She did, however, stand an acceptable distance from Mundo.

Mundo was relating the greatest moment of his life. He said he had once played with a famous Portuguese rock star; he was only eighteen then, my God can you imagine, said Alexandra, shaking her head in wonder. He said he had played in a stadium with thirty thousand people in the audience. He said that words could not describe the exhilaration he felt. My God, said Alexandra. Andrea intertwined her fingers with Mundo's.

Jeffrey said that he once played in a club and a lot of his friends were there, and no, it wasn't the same, but he could guess, then he blushed. Alexandra said that for her it was when she got her letter passing the architecture exam. Her forehead lifted with that continual shock, as if she had just learned the horrible truth.

Alexandra said it was not the same, but Mundo begged to differ. Yes, yes, it's the same, he said. To be an artist is to…etc., etc. He also said that he knew Maria de Medeiros, the actress from *Pulp Fiction* who played Anaïs Nin in *Henry and June*. He said that she liked foosball. They often played together.

"I thought she was French, didn't you think she was French?" Andrea asked Alexandra.

Andrea really did have to use the restroom this time. She excused herself with a lover's glance toward Mundo. The brunette offered Andrea the same weak, awkward smile. The attractive young man stared burningly as she passed.

On her way back, she was abducted by Tanya, who insisted on bringing Andrea to her roommate's small balcony. They had to ball up to step through the windows, and then they stood, just room enough for the two of them and one potted plant. They stood in the delicious night air.

Tanya pointed vaguely, obliquely. She was pointing at sounds. It was gentrified Brooklyn. It was a residential neighborhood and a well-fortified apartment complex. But the sounds of the city always remain. They heard traffic and sirens in the distance. Laughter from the party, some low-playing funk. What it was, though—the sound that would magically distill for any listener—was a click click click a heavy click, expensive things nearly breaking: tile, porcelain, the roll of ivory dice. Tanya put a finger to her lips and waited for a look of understanding in Andrea's face. Andrea's face puzzled and then recognized. Once Andrea latched on to the sound, then Tanya pointed specifically at a building across the street. It was not a gentrified building. It was one of those dinosaurs inhabited by people from previous decades. Not quite level with them, perhaps a floor or two beneath them, they could just make out a handful of Chinese women animatedly playing mahjong. Andrea could see that they were older because a couple of them had grey buns. Their hands moved furiously.

"No matter how loud it is, on Fridays, even with the music all the way up, or when there's traffic, you can hear the tiles."

Andrea felt an intense outburst of affection and grabbed Tanya's hand. She felt like crying. The two of them stood there for a moment, and then Tanya said she was going back in and Andrea said she wanted to stay a moment.

That quality of things about to crack but never cracking, fragile and massive at once. The sound of tile, ivory, porcelain. Old women and their cynical, smoke-deep laughter. What a beautiful thing she could show Mundo after he was done speaking with the artists. The mahjong tiles would be there. The women would play all night, and for a moment, later, she could steal him away.

Andrea thought for a moment of what it would be like to be the princess of Lisbon. She giggled at her girlishness. She thought of what exotic dresses she could wear and then of how Maria de Medeiros would like her as they both had a tomboy streak and yet cultivated a womanly sensuality.

She returned to her place next to Mundo and stood pridefully on his arm. She could see that the entire kitchenful of people was aware of their presence. Three girls in a conversation cluster by the stove would look over every time they experienced a lull, and clearly even

Handsome was getting louder and more aggressive in his jokemaking so that he could be overheard. Andrea told Alexandra she liked her watch and they fondled each other's accessories for a moment. Jeffrey asked Mundo a number of questions—who were his favorite drummers, vocalists. Mundo mentioned that he knew the guitarist from Extreme, that heavy metal band. He said they were Portuguese. They were very famous. The guitarist was a big friend of his. He said it twice: a big friend of his.

A cold sensation gathered at the base of Andrea's skull.

It happened gradually. They kept talking. The brunette excused herself and kissed everybody good night on the cheek, wishing Raimundo particular luck and squeezing his hand. Jeffrey closed in the circle, breathing in largely, pulling up his pants. Mundo said he knew the drummer from "David Letterman." He said he'd traveled to Hong Kong and Singapore and Macao. The cold sensation dispersed evenly through Andrea. She excused herself and went into the living room.

The attractive young man was leaning against the windowsill flipping a coin repeatedly. Andrea arranged herself on the couch for a moment and smoked a cigarette. She crossed her legs higher than was really comfortable and jostled her foot sexily. She gave him until the end of her cigarette, but the attractive young man did not approach her.

She went out to the balcony of Tanya's roommate and smoked another one.

Why Andrea Left Michigan: She was nineteen. She had left the suburbs of Detroit and was spending her days studying a bit and drinking beer and flirting at Michigan State University. She was cute then, but not stunning. Her hair was a burnt orange attempt at blond and she was plump. Still, her nose curved up coyishly and it was the middle of her second year away from home and she made a practice of staying up all night reveling in her freedom. She did all right with boys, met them in the closing hours of the bars, in the never-ending keg lines, developed crushes in the back of lecture halls. It was what she lived for.

She had a best friend who lived for the same reasons; this friend's name was Mandy: Andy and Mandy. Mandy was not from the same suburb, but she was from a similar place. Mandy wore her hair short and for some time had a tail, one long waving strand which wound down her back. They liked woo-woo shots. There was a place to get fries with all sorts of garlic on them and burritos in the middle of the night for a dollar and a half. Mandy never gave up on that slow-paced cashier from State Discount. He carried a skateboard and had a poet's streak.

They were downtown, a six- or seven-block area where there were bookstores and bars and restaurants. A Jean Nicole boutique and an army surplus store. They were on the corner of Abbott and Grand River. There was an ice cream store there. Andrea does not remember the name.

Mandy had a seizure. She fell right to the cement. You could hear it, bone landing on hard surface and she had the face of the dead and her mouth was bubbling and she twitched. Andrea, she didn't do anything. She howled. She stood away. She stepped closer then back, closer then back. Snot ran over Andrea's face as much as tears. People gathered. They made a circle but no one went to Mandy who was flopping like a dying fish.

Andrea made herself do something. She went into the ice cream store and asked them to call 911. She was screaming. A woman, an older woman, thank god, an old hippie woman with her sagging breasts outlined in every detail in that tiny T-shirt, came into the store behind her. Could we have a spoon please? Someone is having a seizure, the woman said—the hippie, her eyes narrowed in concentration. Andrea loved her.

And this is what Andrea would remember: the kid behind the counter with his white paper hat on, he froze, he turned this way and that. He handed the hippie a little plastic spoon. The hippie set the plastic spoon down. She asked instead for the metal spoon sticking in a tin blender cup. She pointed right where it was. *That one there.* You could see the moment in which the kid considered that it was *wrong* to give out the blender-cup spoon. This was against store policy. Then he did.

This is the image which distills for Andrea: the kid staring at the metal spoon and considering.

Then, horror of horrors, when they dashed outside, the hippie said, "Is that your friend, honey?" Andy nodded, bursting with gratefulness. "Here, hold down her tongue." And Andy stood there—she stood six feet away, howling, snot running into her mouth, she could taste it, with the big cold spoon in her hand— while another older woman sat with Mandy and smoothed her hair. The police came.

Andrea never went to the hospital. She made it a few weeks further into the semester, slinking here and there, always moving, talking to no one, and then she remembered an invitation from an old high-school friend. She remembered an old friend from two years earlier who thought college was a waste of time, who had bigger farther-away things to do. A girlfriend with a bit of a desperate look in her eyes, who said *Let's*...

Andrea doesn't have to think about this much anymore. It only *arises* on occasion when she is intensely disliking herself. She sees that kid, his freckles, his absurd plastic spoon, and when it arises she feels a black streak running through her. The twisted, knotted filth which runs through the back of an opaque shrimp. It is supposed to be edible. Here on Tanya's roommate's balcony a million light-years from home or so you'd think. The click of the tiles, massive and fragile at once.

EMBOUCHURE

IT IS NOT supposed to look like this. People should repaint their houses after a few years, when the white goes to yellow or the light blue chips down to the old shade of grey. They should hinge their shutters back up when they come loose on one side, throw the shit off their lawns—the hubcaps and pipes and maybe a torn garden hose. They shouldn't let their sons take on these junkers in the first place. They cost four hundred dollars with a life expectancy of three months and then they rust in the driveway for two years with the hood up, the engine half in, and the other half sitting in pieces nearby.

And then kids will move in, three or four young roommates, and they'll throw cigarette butts and beer cans around until the snow comes, or plastic keg cups, depending on their age and the size of the parties—the younger the larger. One group in that little dark green house on the corner of Potuga and Michigan, two guys and a girl, "just friends," have a wheelchair tipped sideways next to the front porch. They bought it at a junk shop and gave each other rides up and down Potuga and then all three blocks to the Quality Dairy, snickering at their paraplegic act, a forty-ouncer in the girl's lap, up and down the street, laughing until they got bored.

Why should grass die so easily in this part of town? Leave brown spots in the yard like God threw up? What's the use of fences when they're trampled and lie?

Sammy and Genny do the best they can, but the shit starts creeping inside. They spilled coffee on the comforter and it wouldn't come out. The lock on the side door is broken and they've got a stick in it. There was a nice TV before, 36-inch, but it's dead now, and heavy, and they will have to organize four people to help carry it out. The new TV, 24 inches but good color, sits on top of the old. The mirror of the medicine cabinet has cracked and you can't just change the mirror.

Sammy's up on a stepladder with a nail in his mouth, giving the shutter a go, and Gen's sitting on the stoop smoking. He's mad at her anyway.

Genny has two children, one's white and one's Mexican. One is fourteen and one is six and neither of them is Sammy's. Before Sammy, Gen worked weekends too, with the older kid looking after the younger and hating him for it. The older kid making the younger one lick the mud on his motorbike.

Pete is in the yard making army noises for his G.I. Joe. He's the Mexican. He's browner than his father too, and people ask if he's adopted.

"Petie don't be so rough on that doll!" she yells. Sammy looks at her, the first time in hours, and she's sorry that she said "doll."

Her mother named her Genevieve from her high-school French book, but she goes by Genny. No one but her mother called her Genevieve that she can remember, except at the doctor's, or the social security office where they read your name off of documents, or a couple of boyfriends or best friends as a joke.

She is very slim, so that her joints are the largest parts of her limbs, knees bigger than calves and elbows as big as biceps. So she's the only one cold on this warm spring morning. She huddles her legs in under her jean jacket and rocks slightly.

Sammy is short and he's got red hair and freckles and his face is mostly stern. He looks good in blue. He wears it today and his legs are very pale sticking out of his shorts. He looks funny in his sweat socks, so that if it were another time, Gen would tease him about it.

And if it were another time, Genny would answer the phone. She wouldn't sit here on the porch staring out and light another cigarette and listen to it ring. Sammy twists his head and scowls. "You gonna get that?" One side of his mouth is closed down over the nail, so his speech is slurred and he has to say it twice. "You gonna get that?" This is the fourth ring. Gen shakes her head and exhales in a stream. Pete stands up straight to wonder at her. "Pete, go get the phone," Sammy says, and little Pete scrambles to a running start.

"No, no, no. I don't feel like talking." Gen knows it's her mother. Her mother calls on Sunday mornings. Pete stands in front of Genny and looks to her, to her boyfriend, and back, so they can agree and he won't have to pick a side. Sammy gestures with his head back to the spot where Pete was playing and the phone rings once more and then stops.

Gen's sister is Midori after melon liqueur. She goes by Dor. She had a get-together last night. This is what Sammy is all up in arms about.

The two couples—Dor and her husband Jeff, and Gen and Sam—they live near each other and they eat together so often that it's not considered an event. Half the time, they eat what they would have eaten anyway: lasagna, baked chicken, or on a real lazy night, macaroni and hot dogs in front of the TV.

Jeff and Sam get along okay and Gen and Dor are close. Gen is moody and she depends on Dor to tell her when she's overstepping that line. Lots of times, Gen wants too much too fast and she pisses people off. When it comes to promotions, she asks, why not me? If she doesn't like her birthday present, she won't pretend otherwise.

Dor will tell her it's just not worth it, that Sam can too go out without her two Fridays in a row, or when to call their mother and apologize. Gen takes a deep breath and says yeah, yeah you're right. Dor is the even-tempered one, the one who bites her tongue. That's why bosses like Dor and she gets promoted. She's management and makes good money.

Dor tries to help and Gen does try to listen. Sometimes, though, she is such a brat. Gen ruins things and there's no stopping her. Anyone who knows her can see it coming. She starts rolling her eyes. She's picked an enemy.

The get-together should have been nice. They had an extra couple and that made it a party. Jeff had run into an old friend from high school. The old friend brought his wife, and they were all ready to laugh easily and make jokes out of whatever popped into their heads.

They had wild rice soup and ribs with so much barbeque sauce that they ate with their fingers spread and upright. Jeff made a crack about sterilized doctors that lasted quite a while. They said "scalpel" for knife and "incoming" from "M*A*S*H." Sammy brought lots of beer and a couple of wine coolers for his sister-in-law who prefers something sweet. Dori said the lemon meringue took hours and hours and then "to thaw" into her fist like she was coughing. It should have been a nice get-together except Gen decided she hated Ned and Trish, the real guests, the ones who made the party, the ones the others were ready to laugh for. Gen barely looked at them and kept her face wrinkled and made it uncomfortable for everybody.

Sure, Trish was trying too hard. She was full of unnecessary noises, sighs and giggles. She said "ooooo" like the high-pitched squeeze of a baby toy. This might grate on anyone, but they made allowances. Trish was only twenty-three, and she was nervous, and who cares anyway? It was just one little get-together. She and Ned were visiting from out of town, and they'd never see her again.

It could have been Ned. Ned and Gen had a thing twenty years ago, the summer she was fifteen and he was twenty. That was a big deal back then. Five of them knew about it—everyone but Trish. But it would be silly if that were what it was all about now. It's a pretty small town and people have tried various combinations and met back up again in different pairs and known how to act. Dor went to Christmas dance with Sammy junior year of high school. They're about the same age. It just happens that way. So Midori and Sam and Jeff were at a loss. From where did this *attitude*, this anger in motion, come?

Ned had come in from out of town, and no one had seen him for at least a dozen years. Gen hadn't seen him in twenty. Ned and Jeff had played hockey together. Ned and Trish were visiting his folks and they met Jeff getting gas at the Shell station and they got to talking about hockey initiation, how they shaved off one of your eyebrows. Ned said how it worked because you were so humiliated everywhere except with the people with one eyebrow too and the team became everything. Jeff said, yeah, yeah, you're right, and then he said my wife Dor—you know Dori Taylor?—her sister is coming over why don't you come too and Ned said he didn't know Dor really, but he knew Gen. And he said sure.

Trish was the loser from the start. She was not from these people and they made her nervous. Genny hated her all the more for not fighting back. Trish's hair was scalp-short on one side and then splashed down auburn over the other ear. She ate with a hand over her mouth, like someone would snatch the food away.

Trish went to the bathroom and Gen said something about the pitch of the young woman's voice, dolphins all over the world would get horny, and everyone laughed, including Trish's husband, but not including Dor, who shot her sister a scolding glance. They were still laughing when Trish got back, so she asked what? what? and no one would answer.

Genny made noises too. For every shrill chirp, she did something guttural. Trish was like trapped air fighting for the slightest relief, just enough off the top to sustain pressure without bursting. Gen was like the whole thing letting loose at once—guffaws, snorts and the thud of her hands on the table.

Gen made no attempt to hide her irritation. She winced when Trish spoke, rolled her eyes. The madder Gen got, the higher Trish's voice became, like someone was twisting her, pinching. She blushed.

Ned seemed oblivious to his wife's embarrassment. He was always looking somewhere else when she spoke or was spoken to. He kept a hand over hers, would pat it every once and a while. He studied the home, looked high, at the curtain rods, or where the ceiling met the walls. Like he was watching a plane in the distance. He studied high when Trish had attention, and when it was over, he asked about pictures and old times. Dori's photo collage hung in the living room: When was this of Dor and Gen taken? Where? Was this a cousin, an uncle? You still friends with so-and-so? Isn't that so-and-so's sister? These are Gen's kids? Well, I'll be damned. Beautiful boys. How old is the oldest?

He asked Jeff about their classmates: County *what* officer? Obese? No kidding. Jeff listed the greatest oddities, most kids, most divorces, still together, celebrity newscaster, jail. Ned's black beard grew half way over his cheeks and made his face look very long and thin. His grey disguised him too, and you really would not know him as the young man unless you knew him well. He still had that way, though. He'd study you with eyes narrowed for a second and then he'd be in space and make you feel boring.

Everything Ned said, Trish had to make a *"we"* of. Ned said he hated groceries; Trish said, "Oh, we never shop for groceries." Ned said he drank a pot of coffee every day; "At least two," Trish chirped and then nodded.

Gen went to do dishes in the kitchen, insisted, no no no, let me. She hoped to defuse herself, find a moment of peace with the water running. By the time she got down to the silverware, she felt less irritable. She put the last fork prong-up in the plastic rack and grabbed a beer out of the fridge. She swigged. Dor came in, grabbed three beers and her wine cooler, and gave her sister the once-over.

"I'm just gonna have a cigarette."

Dor nodded. "Thanks for doing the dishes." She was satisfied that the strangeness was over.

Gen smoked and leaned a hip against the sink. Her face went blank. This is when she looks most like her sister. Otherwise their expressions separate them. Gen's face looks more muscular because she's always tense—the pinched forehead, the squirming outline of her jaw. Dor has more flesh. Her eyes are relaxed and look bigger. She smiles with both sides of her mouth.

Gen butted out her cigarette and threw it away and cleaned the ashtray. She wiped up the kitchen, left the kettle and the broiler pans soaking.

Gen does things quickly and she's sloppy. She's good at getting things done but she doesn't do it carefully. If she says today is the day for Christmas cards, she'll mail out every last one, but notes will be insultingly short and a few will come back without stamps or with the wrong address. So Dori's kitchen was not clean the way Dor herself would like. There was lipstick on a glass and a few grains of rice everywhere, the underside of a bowl, the floor, the back of the sink. But it was clean enough for Gen. Finishing is the thing.

Just when she closed her eyes and felt her headache cooling, Trish came in with a little saucer, a bite or two of lemon meringue left. She also had her beer. She brought her beer like she was staying a while.

Genny raised her chin and watched. She folded her arms. "Hi," Trish said, and smoothed the short side of her hair. Genny did not answer.

Defending herself was not something Trish considered. She

would not shrug at this moment or say "suit yourself." She didn't think of leaving, or ignoring or questioning Gen's hostility. From the moment she walked in the door, she wanted the pair of sisters, these expanded and contracted, shorter or quicker, kinder and softer or more taut versions of each other, to like her.

Dor was easy. But Gen hated her, and no moment more than when she walked into the kitchen trying again. Why did she care? The dessert dishes were all still out—why bring one saucer in? Why be so obvious, bring the beer along? Gen hated Trish because she was twenty-three, a very young twenty-three, *infantile*. And you could assume, with this type of girl, that no tragedy had happened. No love then him leaving, no car wrecks, no labor, children or horrible guilt. No betrayal, no *you are like dead to me*. Her grandparents were probably still alive. Genny hated her for being weak and marrying a man who ignored her. And at the core, most and worst, there was Gen's own up-washing shame. So that when Trish set her saucer in the sink and looked up to make conversation, considered her words, an offer to help or a comment on the food, she didn't get a chance.

Gen shook her head and sneered. "Are you just gonna leave that in there? Jesus!" like, *How could you?* She washed the saucer quickly and stuffed it in the rack.

"I'm sorry, I mean, I just wasn't thinking…" Trish was panicking, bending her knees. Gen wanted to throttle her, slap her or do *violence*. Instead, she stormed out.

She said, "You're so fuckin' squeaky," with her hands flailing and her teeth set to spit, but with her back turned and hurrying away like a coward. She banged through the get-together out to the front porch to take a few deep breaths and keep herself from crying. Sam apologized to everyone and then yanked her home.

It felt like she was playing on tissue paper. She felt like she was spitting dry, pp—pph—ph, to get lint off her lip. The clarinet was hissing. It was not making notes because her lips were clumsy and the
reed was soft. She paused. She pulled the instrument against her chest
crossways. The TV buzzed quietly in the outer room. Dori would
turn it down when she practiced. Dori knew she was practicing.

It would be like starting over. She would have to tap loudly, one-
two-three-four, an audible tap, not a toe scrunching or a mental
beat, but an audible tap like in sixth grade. One-two-three-four.
Start over and with the right reed this time. This time the reed is
soft and she must not bite on her lips. She must be gentle, but
stern, in control, flexible, like a parent wants to be. She places her
fingers and taps. One single note, a C. C is the first thing you learn.
A spaceship beneath the clef, three holes covered and no keys, no
sharps or flats, a baby note. That is easy, that is clear, and she
moves up D-E-F, a slow and easy scale. Her lips are clumsy but the
slow easy scale is possible. On to half notes, and then quarter and
then eighth and then problems, and then she is years back, and
then she plays like in the beginning, with hisses and sputters and
lint spit.

Her *Advanced Method Rubank* book is open to "Two Minuets." This is where she should be. *Dolce*, A-flat, B-flat, E-flat, sixteenth notes. This is where she was before the soft reed. *Allegretto non tanto e con grazia*. Her saliva is everywhere. She places the instrument on the bed, not in its case, and opens the door to Midori and the TV.

"Hi," says Dor. She's curled up in front of the couch. Gen slaps her thigh and she scootches over. The house is dark but it's afternoon.

"Where's Mom?"

"Out with Caroline—buyin' shoes."

"Shoes?" says Gen. Shoes are that much less toward the new clarinet. Her mother promised her a Buffet for high school. A used Buffet would be good enough, but even that would take some planning, and it was July, half way through the summer, and she has seen no approaching new used Buffet.

"Shoes?" And the way she says it, Dori starts crying for her.

Miss Gerald came to her fourth-hour music class and watched the ninth graders. Genny was proud. Mr. Anders, the junior-high teacher, stood beaming over her solo, wands wide and furious. Genny's music was big. There were nine clarinets, half the junior-high band, and Gen was first chair and played the solo. Everyone else had to place their instruments across their laps and wait to come back in. She honked once, up there on a high note, but it didn't matter, because she was swelling and Mr. Anders' wands and Miss Gerald's attention were hers.

Miss Gerald was young for a teacher and her legs were short, so that only her toes touched the floor as she sat facing them. Her hair was blond and straight and parted in the middle, and she clasped her hands behind her neck so that her elbows stuck out like a double set of breasts. She studied Genny. You could tell she was studying Genny. Her eyes swept over from section to section—one flute, three sax, two trumpets, the trombone and percussion—watching hands and mouths, but it was Gen she paused to consider, Gen's solo when she curled a finger under her chin.

The bell rang and everyone stood up to pack—unhitch, place away. Mr. Anders touched Gen's arm. He nodded and smiled. Miss Gerald wanted to talk to her. She gestured to leave the clarinet out, and the three of them made a triangle around Gen's music stand. Gen flushed—adrenaline like just before the solo. Mr. Anders placed a hand on his pride and joy's shoulder.

"Genny Taylor... This is Miss Gerald."

Gen scratched one ankle with the other and mouthed hello. She held her instrument behind her back, like surprise flowers for a date. Miss Gerald said hello and looked at the floor until Mr. Anders realized she wanted him gone.

"Excuse me," he said, puzzled and shutting the door.

"You're a very good clarinetist for your age."

"Thank you." Gen was meek.

"Are you going to try out for high-school concert band?" Miss Gerald looked at the tip of her boot.

"Oh yes."

Genny moved her. She reminded her of herself, frail and aggressive at once. She wouldn't be like other girls. She would be like Miss Gerald at her age: Unlike.

There was a problem. "Gen, would you do me a favor and play a low B-flat?" Gen poised and blew. "Now play staccato." Gen's staccato was her weak point. She could not get it clean enough. It did not go from clear tone to an instant of nothing and back. There was always sound leftover, entangled.

Gen grew hot, felt like she needed the bathroom. Miss Gerald would have taken her hand if she knew her any better. "That's what I thought. See, honey, you've got a problem that causes a whole set of problems. You could be first chair next year, but you've got to fix your *embouchure*. Your reed is too hard, so your *embouchure* is too tense. You don't have any control. You don't have a clean attack.

Your reed is so hard, you have to bite." Miss Gerald imitated, her lips turned white. Gen was hot on the outside and her innards went chilly.

"It's a pretty common problem for musicians your age. Lots of times, people play on a harder reed because it's a quick way to a stronger sound. But you need a reed you can control. Your flats are not true half steps . . ."

Miss Gerald gave her a list: change reeds and therefore change *embouchure*, smile up at the corners—see? She said, get a better clarinet than this junior high's *Godknowswhere*-it's-been piece of crap. She said, take private lessons—a ninety-minute drive to the college, every other week, if it had to be. And she loved Gen, and she said, Genevieve, you are good, better than just first chair, high school; you could go on and go far away.

Mrs. Taylor said yes yes yes, the Buffet, and private lessons too. But Mrs. Taylor said a lot of things.

Mrs. Taylor never expected this form of rebellion. She was prepared for something else altogether, reveled in her readiness. She had two girls, thank god, and she knew how to compromise, unlike her own mother. They would have curfews, but the curfews would be late, and when boys picked them up, they would not have to come and sit in the living room under scrutiny so that they would be afraid to come back. They could use make-up whenever they wanted. They could wear whatever they wanted. They could drink beer within reason, and she smoked herself, so what could she say? She would be willing to buy them pretty things. They would enjoy prettiness for as long as they could, before they had to work and their hair went greasy with sweat. Boys would come offering things, stuffed animals from bull's-eye games, hidden pints of whiskey. *Be careful*, she'd say. Hickeys would not bother her. They would not get pregnant. But this? Genevieve in her room honking, honking and crying over the honks? Genevieve, who may not have kissed anyone at this age? Genevieve, whose hair was greasy with indifference anyway, skinny and plain on purpose?

Two steps forward, three back. If only she could reverse the proportion. That is the goal. That is why she sits in her chair, the windowsill for a music stand, instrument over her knees, trying to cry quietly. Silent so that Dori won't cry with her and her mother won't ask why. Like trying to catch a scurrying animal in one hand—the pressure of her lips is an operation that precise and elusive. If she does not have this, what does she have?

Vicki McGee lives around the corner, and Genny can see her back yard from the bathroom window. Vicki and her friend Joanne are always tanning. Genny tries to watch with just one eye and no face showing so they'll never know she's there. They lie on towels in the tall grass, scratch themselves, giggle, and smoke. They do their nails. Every once and a while, the phone rings and Vicki will go in the screen door, then come back out swinging her hair and pulling her bikini down over her behind. Her bikini is tiny and she's stacked. Guys come over and smoke too, and there's something unnerving about the way they sit in their jeans and T-shirts, a kitchen chair dragged out back, sitting with the girls half-naked and lying down. Joanne and Vicki make no move to cover themselves. Vicki arches her back. The guys sometimes rub in the lotion. Once, Joanne made out on a towel with the running back while Vicki flipped through a magazine alone and next to them, the transistor crackling.

Ned lived nearby too. He went to college and came home for the summer. He hated everything about it. There was nothing to do but drink. He had to pump gas. He counted the days. He would work and come home and shut the door to his room. He read all his books in the first three weeks, and then the library was a joke. After that, he watched TV, but it gets hotter and hotter and he could only take so much. One night, he finally went out drinking with an old high-school buddy, and the next day, he was walking home and saw Genny Taylor sitting on her front stoop.

She had the face of an old woman, but you could tell she was a girl. Her nose and ears and cheekbones were large, out of proportion to the rest of her face, like features she had shrunk away from or would grow into. She huddled into herself. Ned's hands smelled like gas, his hair was stuck together in clumps. He couldn't rub his itching cheek for fear of making everything worse.

He saw her and knew about the rest of his summer. He wanted to shower and come back to the same moment, pass by again in fresh socks, clear of splotches, grease and sticky spots. Scrape off whatever filth ran in a line from the back of his neck to his ass. The last time he remembered Gen Taylor, she was running to the Dairy for her mother, pulling her sister by the wrist. She still had a girlish body, still chestless and too small for her feet, but there was something in her expression that brought her into Ned's realm of interest.

She was lost in thought, gazing at nothing worth looking at, eyebrows raised like she was determining something awful. It was her mouth, though. She was neither smiling nor frowning, moving no muscle beneath her nose, and yet her lips seemed to throb. Her lips became larger then again smaller, had a life of their own. This was the only thing stirring for moments. Then she'd throw her head back like, God Please, and inhale deeply and go back to staring with the pulse of her lips. Ned swore he saw her tongue flicker.

It happened in her own mother's bedroom. At first she didn't have anything to tell him. He said she was pretty. She said her name was Genny with a g and not a j. He had very dark hair, like black shoe-polish dye or the darkest of blueberries. She sat at the head of the bed and he rubbed her fingers and she went liquid.

Their slightly open mouths were just sad enough for sweet. He laid a towel over the bedspread. She was scared. He said, what's the difference if I touch you here, or here, or here? She knew before it started that she would, though.

He said, please? Then it hurt so bad that she looked over her shoulder at the clock. It could only be so many minutes. Dori knocked on the door and said, "Gen?" Gen said to leave them alone. She would try to get him to leave by the back door. She could kiss him good-bye at the back door where Vicki and Joanne might see.

PURE IMPENDING GLORY

I

THE STORY AT HAND

WHEN OUR young professor was in graduate school, she worked weekends for a catering company. This was often quite humiliating. Not so much because of the uniform or the silver-haired mothers of the bride who found the always imperfect flunkies a good way to exercise their nerves. It didn't bother her so much when the publicity coordinator of an arts organization would complain about the improper presentation of tiny quiches or the poorly timed entrance of cream cheese and salami. What used to really get to our heroine was her invisibility.

Her first defense was to sound as cultured or as educated as possible. She would answer simple questions in a lecturer's voice, self-consciously enunciative. "Why certainly, the path to the loo might be explained." She attempted small talk. "Goodness, it is terribly cold in here," she said, approximating something of New England. The response was a nod or a weak smile.

It was important to her that these people acknowledge her.

During a spring wedding, she attempted to make friends with a disheveled outcast cousin. She figured she could work her way in from there. If he would strike up a conversation with her, perhaps others could be brought in as well. This was against the caterer's policy, but it was imperative that she be recognized.

Our promising young scholar eavesdropped and learned that the cousin's name was Sammy. He was a short, slight man with hair that reached out at various angles. His suit pants were so ill-fitting that the whites of his pockets showed. He smoked cigars.

The Learned Waitress felt it was safe to assume he would hate this sort of ceremony and wanted to enter into conspiracy with him.

"Long speeches, huh?" she whispered, as he perused the deviled eggs. Sammy was quite drunk and straining to breathe around his congestion. It took him a moment to realize who was speaking to him. He looked around at first, and then met our heroine's eyes. He exhaled liquidly and patted his jacket, searching for his handkerchief. He blew his nose. He nodded. He selected an egg.

This was when she began resorting to her third and longest lasting method of defense. She was furious and she watched as the outcast cousin hobbled off. The thin and poorly formed runt of the extended family, and she thought to herself, *I could kick his ass.*

Now, our young graduate student had never fought in her life. She was from a relatively poor section of a small Midwestern city, but it was hardly impoverished, hardly as violent as our city's centers often are, and it was easy to get around the occasional cat fights which took place among her peers. She had, once or twice, resorted to acting tougher than she was, yelling at a threatening young lady, but mostly kept to herself and stayed out of trouble. She had never pulled anybody's hair outside the family nor threatened any teen's beauty with her nails.

And so it began. The graduate student, whenever she felt slighted, be it a 6´2˝ model or a seventy-four-year-old patroness, would brace herself, would peer back boldly into people's eyes by telling herself, gritted teeth not necessary, *I could kick this bitch's ass.*

She was short and just a bit thick. Long hours on her feet and carrying trays kept her in shape. If her nemeses were sizable, she told herself she was stronger by will, would fight dirty if necessary.

She never struck anybody nor mentioned her intentions.

Eventually, she obtained an assistantship, and no longer had to suffer constant professional invisibility, but she never completely left off resorting to this method.

She kept its use to a minimum for many years, but the first year of her appointment at the small college, she found this anger resurging.

It is an added misery to teach when one is depressed, to be responsible for others and to be good, in the moral sense, as teachers are expected to be. It struck her as cruel and unusual that she must be even-tempered and of unusually high integrity. After all, she had not chosen parenthood. Her students' vulnerability frightened and disturbed her. They would approach with their half-folded papers and their redundant questions (*I mentioned that earlier. Get the notes from a classmate. Didn't you get the handout?*). Their nerves, their wavering voices—she felt it to be an indictment of her position, the tyranny. She was an ogre of a father and they were coming begging for permission, fearing her random temper. Their fear was the indictment. She resented that they cared so much what she thought, that there would be ramifications to her mistakes. She was always angry. That year she was tense, cringing and always angry. A few times, two or three times, when students argued over grades, and her grades were untypically stern that year, she explained herself defensively and said to herself, if it came down to it, *I could kick...*

About this time, our young professor (Doctor Capistrano—her name) made a trip to the bank. It seemed they were short-handed and she had been waiting quite some time, ten minutes longer than expected, and she, along with all the other patrons, was wondering if she could complete the necessary errands within the given time. She stood there in her smart little pants suit, arms folded, exhaling violently through her nose. She, like everybody else, would lean to the side occasionally and peer down the winding, roped-in queue, as if something might have changed since the last time. She, like everybody else, would scowl, look at her watch, and shake her head.

They made an announcement. They opened another window for deposits only, which was all the good doctor had to do. As she moved forward, she noticed that no one in front of her seemed to be relieved by the news. She would be next, and then she saw a young woman, a young bohemian, a white girl, a punk rocker with over-dyed red hair and holes in her clothes, she saw this girl, smaller and slighter than she, duck through the ropes, come from behind and duck through the ropes to get to the window first.

"Oh Miss," Capistrano said, "I was here…" but even as she began to speak she knew it was too late. She could see in the girl's body language that she had heard, but chosen to ignore.

Our heroine was next up. She finished quickly and turned to find the punker walking slowly out of the bank. Dr. C was enraged. She told herself what she could do, and more than ever, wanted the girl to know that the good doctor had the power to exercise her anger.

Dr. C walked closely and swiftly behind the girl. She walked closely enough to kick the child's heels with each step. The girl turned around once and then darted away.

Later when our young professor, who shall henceforth also be referred to by her Christian name Maya, reflected on this moment, she was supremely disgusted with herself. Her fury was ridiculous,

and the woman was young enough, bohemian enough, in all likeli-
hood, to be a student at the college. She could show up in one of
Maya's classes.

Maya was resolutely ashamed and promised to be better, but, as
we all know, when we are in that downward spiral, we can do nothing right. We slide into shelves and reach for lamps to steady ourselves. We lose our jobs and drive our spouses away. We say *I hate
you. No, I mean help me.* The undesirable shove forward their faces
with hot and rancid breath until there is nobody left (for what is
more undesirable than need?)—or if we are of a defensive nature,
we withdraw first. We sit in the dark on the edge of our beds, staring at the backs of our hands and lamenting that no one has tried
hard enough to find us.

And so, although the banking incident led Maya to resolve to be
a better human being, she was simply too far gone. Only terrific
luck might raise confidence in the middle of the downward spiral.
Only terrific luck may change one's direction. And then on the way
up, we can do no wrong. The only problem is that terrific luck
arrives only every so often. And then again, on the way down we
may not recognize terrific luck, or we grasp at it and our aim is
absurd. Our hands land instead upon lamps.

Dr. C promised to try harder, to make some friends, be better.

We join her late one winter evening after a party. She had left
the party too early, and so she was exponentially lonely. She had
been enjoying herself. She had liked many of the people around her.
She had, at several moments, felt herself to be *one of* them. She had
touched Dr. Chandran, of the Linguistics Department, lovingly on
the arm while they laughed. Dr. Chandran was the only other
woman of our heroine's age, closer to thirty than forty. Dr.
Chandran, always the punster, had accused her of being "Ed-
McMahon-ic," and though this embarrassed the party of the first

part, somewhat, as being a self-consciously clever joke (she had heard this before), she laughed with her eyes squeezed shut, with an appropriate irony.

Dr. Capistrano also had a love for Dr. Chandran because Dr. Ch was an immigrant, while Dr. C was from an immigrant family. Dr. C always looked up to immigrants as being older and wiser, as having experienced things at which she could only guess, and a mentorship would be ideal for this period of her life.

Dr. C had needed Dr. Ch's friendship so badly that it scared her and so she left the party early. And here was Dr. C standing before the phone, trying to imagine which of her distant friends might be home on a Friday night. She had a white wine in her hand and she laughed at the ridiculousness of it—the first time she felt she had a friend on this little campus out in the middle of nowhere and then it was as if she'd become so addicted to loneliness that she could not resist its call.

Her hair was in a bun, as always. Her suit was rather stark. Capistrano looked a great deal younger than she was and worked to appear professional. She had had enough to drink that her white wine swirled while she was supposedly standing still.

By this time, she felt that she had two friends left in the world.

Madam X had been Maya's friend for nearly twenty years. They had worked at a pizza place for several summers in a row, back in that mid-sized, industrial, Midwestern city. Together, they discovered that the hierarchies of their high school fell away in a different part of town. They reveled in their new identities and flirted outrageously with any masculine form whatsoever. They flirted with the cooks and delivery men and the workers who came in for a slice during lunch break. Madam X was short and dark like Dr. C. Madam X had huge, pretty black eyes. Their relationship had not much changed in twenty years. They talked about men. Madam X had been through one marriage and several married men. After she spoke with X, C was often angry with herself. All they had left in common was a desire to be loved. Dr. C had had no recent romances so she had kept referring back to the same old stories in order to give the conversation any balance whatsoever.

X worked in the financial aid office of a community college not far from where they grew up. Every once and a while they would talk about the current fashions of young people, and then X would go back to sex and C would listen or participate. X had slept with a struggling sophomore. He didn't have a dollar for the bus home. C repeated the one about the much older man she had met while she was an undergraduate. He had been chinless and nervous, but she liked how it felt to sit in his expensive and smoothly rolling sports car. Every time C hung up, she felt she had degraded herself, and yet she could think of nothing else to discuss and only one other person to call.

Madam Y was also a professor and a writer. She still lived in the city which Dr. C had left the previous year. With Madam Y, there was a gamble. Sometimes when C called Y, there was a distant harassed sound in her voice. She didn't like to just talk. She was busy. It should be important.

Maya had, for quite some time, sensed her remaining friendships disintegrating. She had left the city expecting to maintain more than two by means of phone, at least, expecting to make a few here or there amongst the faculty of the little, Eastern, reasonably respected, but not outstanding, college. (She was young, she could make the big time by forty-five. This was the kind of place considered a steppingstone by most all of its faculty, and those who had not stepped further were a touch sour.)

Professor Maya Capistrano had ceased calling many of her old friends from the city. She knew it was a phase, but she was easily hurt, and Donna argued with her too much and Alexa was running around with Umberto to fabulous parties in the film industry, and Dr. C knew this too would pass, but it made her wistful for her youth. Wistful is perhaps not strong enough a word. Jealous might be more accurate. It made her anxious that she had not taken advantage of her time.

Madam X was always consistent. Madam X was there no matter the weather and always glad to speak to Madam C even if they could speak of nothing important to C. And Madam Y—they had, C and Y, at one time been so close, enjoyed such kinship, that Maya would now withstand this discomfort until her faith returned and they could be close again. (C finished her dissertation one year after Y and began her novel the following year. Y had written two works of fiction—one collection of stories and a novel afterward.)

Which brings us not to *it*, but to a major precipitator of the story at hand. An event which Maya would argue had been crucial to the next phase of her life.

Soon after leaving the city, Maya had sold her novel. She sold it to a press so small and obscure that she was more embarrassed than anything at the news. It was not an academic press, but an underground collective which dealt with many New Age works. Madam Y and Madam C had once joked together, back in the days of their deep affection and implicit understanding, of selling works to "Rat's Ass Press."

This was not funny.

Maya spoke with the editor and felt a slight rush of adrenaline. She didn't hang completely up, but pressed the "reset" button on her receiver and began to call every one she knew. She told her parents first, who were excited and proud. She told Madam X who shrieked and whistled. She left messages for Donna and Alexa, but was able to catch Madam Y in person, who immediately asked her, "What press?"

Y had sold her own books, through an agent, to a major house. Maya told her the name of the house, and Madam Y sighed with recognition. "That's terrific," Y said, in the manner, our friend would describe, of a mother to daughter's crayon project.

C, anticipating Y's lack of respect, felt the need to concur. So she made fun of the editor, who was high-pitched, tentative and easily manipulated. "I could get my way with a carefully placed silence." Y laughed too hard. C could not wait to get off the phone.

C bristled. She was beaten and humiliated. And later, much later, if you were to ask her how the whole thing started, the story about to be told, she might say that she was depressed about her book and looking for comfort.

She wouldn't mention her violent urges in the bank or say that she had left the party too early, that it had been one of the lonelier weekends of her stay. That the opportunities she had longed for—Dr. Chandran, for example—were only taunting her. She stood before the phone. Her white wine was too cold, but Maya drank it anyway and let it do unnerving things to her teeth.

The good doctor called X, who received her warmly and had a number of stories to tell. Dr. C gathered her stocking feet up into her desk chair and huddled in the dark.

Being a fighter, on Monday Dr. Capistrano woke with resolve. She would take her life into her own hands. She had learned at some point—would relearn and forget and relearn—that she could make herself feel better by making others feel good first. She would bestow kindness upon those who were even more nervous than she. Perhaps she was too frightened to go visiting Chandran two floors down, but there was a shy young composition instructor she could ask about his weekend. And if she chanced upon Chandran in the halls, Maya could greet her warmly, with enthusiasm.

Dr. C decided it was time to take a lover. Not a love—she was far too vulnerable for that—but a lover, a nice man with whom she had nothing in common. A business man who liked her for her looks, a FedEx man who would find it thrilling to put a professor on his résumé.

She would joke with and tease her students. No more of this adolescent assumption that everyone but she knew the incomprehensible rules.

It was a brisk morning. She wore her hair down for the first time in her six months in the place. She walked to work, stepping quickly in these last days of winter. She wanted to open herself up to as many people as possible. She grinned to herself, though she was more unhappy than anything, because she felt perhaps someone would speak to her if she looked approachable. She was aware of looking like a girl and wanted to flirt with a stranger. She stopped for a cup of coffee in the diner, preened before the cook and went unnoticed, but the gas station attendant smiled shyly as she passed, with a slight puffing of the cheeks.

"Lady Chatterly," Y had called C, because C preferred lovers who worked with their hands. Y had never understood the fascination (What do you talk about?) but C had felt the situation was natural. The pool of men of color, academics at this particular institution, was very small and reduced even further by those who preferred white women. Her preference for brown superseded her preference for intellect. Such were the circumstances, that she often had to choose between them.

And, in her moments of insecurity, she didn't feel her advanced education to be a natural part of her. It was somehow superimposed. What C understood—the forces which brought her to academia were capricious forces. 1) Her parents happened to move into the one low-income neighborhood near the best public schools in their industrial Midwestern city. Most everyone else attending these schools came from more money, which was painful on one level, *but,* 2) Maya had an outstanding ear. From a very small age, she could imitate with amazing accuracy. She could recall the melody of a song heard months before and break everyone up with an exact replica of the landlord's intonation. Maya was able to imitate her teachers' speech patterns and therefore learned the language of the middle class. She then was accepted by a good college and learned the language of academics. She excelled as an undergraduate and went on to an exceptional graduate school. X, Maya's childhood friend, also from the only low-income etc., though hard-working and inspired, did not have such an ear. X had a stubborn ear, and though she made it through a state school with flying colors, she had not had the sense of accomplishment of our young professor.

So here is Maya with her girlish hair down, walking briskly to the campus, approximating, she felt in particular on this day, a professor of comparative literature. She would be teaching the latter part of *Notes From the Underground* and knew she could entertain her students with a theatrical interpretation of sputtering resentment. It was a day of potential.

THE FORM THEIR RITUAL SHOULD TAKE

For most of her working life, Maya has felt quite asexual on campus. She finds herself in a different body. Her walk loses all lateral movement whatsoever. There is perhaps a slight vertical bounce, and when she sits, she finds that she is constantly trying to contain herself. She crosses her arms over her chest, holds the opposite biceps and squeezes.

And so here we find Maya coming from the street with her naughty grin, her slight lateral movement, and if we are patient, we should be able to perceive a change in temperament. We should notice her become the contemplative professional, her vocabulary more complex, her carriage authoritative. We should see this—most days we would have seen this—but here we are now, very close to the story at hand, and again it could be argued that the decision not to stiffen on this particular day, the earlier decision to wear her girlish hair down, are major precipitators of *it*. She said hello to a secretary winding up the stairs of Burcham Hall toward the fourth-floor Comp Lit Department. The younger woman mouthed hello uncomfortably back, obviously not recognizing Maya, and then did a double take. Incidents of this nature continued to occur. Steven, the Existentialism Guy, squinted from his corner office. A student's timing was a little off in response.

Maya stopped in the mail room to use the copy machine. She needed twenty-five copies of a critical essay. This would be a lengthy operation, so she got started before she even took off her coat. She pressed the sorter and the machine made horrible plastic clunks. She opened the book to the last page, set it all up, and proceeded copying while she unwound her purse and set her jacket over a chair. She was on the second page when Philip, Mr. British Intellectual History, entered.

He was a big man. He was nearly a foot taller than Maya and he dressed rather casually compared to the others. He wore jeans and a tie, and over that, a red-and-black-plaid lumberjack coat. He was a big man with a gentle concerned voice. His hair was salt and pepper. He was a bit pear-shaped, hips wider than shoulders.

Part of it was that Maya always felt the need to speak with as complex a usage as possible around any of her colleagues. She looked twenty-four, especially with her girlish hair down, and colleagues had a way of speaking to her as if she were much younger than they. As if she were a student. They used their loud lecture voices and disagreed readily.

She was armed with Latinates. Philip seemed to be anxious. He watched her set up, and stood leaning against the water cooler with a set of papers folded before him.

"Are you desirous…" Dr. C began, "…of the Xerox machine?" She paused for a breath after "desirous."

Philip's blue eyes widened and his smile was open, without teeth. "Desirous?" he repeated.

Maya felt she had crossed a line. Her rush of embarrassment quickly became a thrill. Philip was flustered. Philip collected himself. "Just a couple of copies." And then he did not again glance at Ms. Dr. Prof. Capistrano until he was leaving the room.

And then Maya could not help herself. She felt herself to be in a new realm where the understood undocumented rules of conduct were unimportant, were beneath her.

Maya went back to her office, turned her chair around, and sat down on it backwards. She hugged the back of the seat between her knees, as a cellist her beloved instrument. Her slacks inched up so that there was space between her socks and the hem. She liked the feel of this unusual exposure in the chill air. She licked her finger unnecessarily and flipped through some papers.

She had made two appointments with students who were in danger of failing. Paula was a smart girl who was extremely lazy or distracted. She wrote an outstanding in-class essay at the beginning of the course and then stopped doing the reading all together. For the last month she had handed in vague papers only obliquely related to the text. The last one had been composed by pen, obviously while using some form of transportation.

Kirk was also coming. He was a cringing young man who wrote papers half the required length. He never took off his coat in class, nor looked up from his desk. He wasn't doing the reading either.

Paula came first. The girl was a fashion plate. She wore her hair lifted and pinned in back, two strands carefully hanging. Her eyebrows were impeccably plucked. The student started when she first saw Maya with her rakish chair turned, but this surprise quickly gave way to shame. She knew why she was there, and sat down demurely with her eyes lowered.

"You know why you're here?" Maya asked and Paula nodded, and then Maya told her what to do to pass, and then Maya said, "Woman to woman, Paula—you're a cute girl. You probably get a lot of attention. Don't just rely on your looks." As she said this last part, Maya leaned in toward the girl and the girl leaned back and laughed awkwardly. Maya put her hand on Paula's shoulder as she walked her to the door.

Kirk was standing out in the hall, leaning against the wall. He held his backpack as if it were a loose stack of books, to his chest carefully.

"The doctor will see you now," Maya said, it might be argued, sexily. Kirk responded with a smile which was quite close to a wince. She gestured toward his seat and shut the door. Maya spared him the backward seat, and instead sat down on her own hands.

"Obviously, you're capable of much more than this," etc., etc. Our lovely Dr. C scolded him without the use of gesture, as her hands were restrained. Kirk began to sweat on the sides of his face. He sweat in the place where sideburns would be. He grimaced. His eyes were continually shrinking.

When he adopted an expression of thorough squeamishness, she showed him to the door.

Our darling professor chuckled. She nibbled at an eraser, placed her feet on her desk, found this uncomfortable and set her feet back down on the floor.

We are very close, now, to the story at hand. This is where Antonio comes in.

Let us make this perfectly clear: Antonio was not in her class at the time. He had been in her class the previous semester. And yet she was not surprised to see him. She had expected this.

It would be a lie to say she had not noticed him. Yet her intentions were not admitted until this particular day.

Antonio was a Black Cuban. He was tall and thin and handsome, with golden eyes and plump pink lips. He looked no older
than he was, twenty or twenty-one, except that he was perhaps a
touch more graceful than others in the final stages of adolescence.

He had immigrated as a young teenager, so that his accent was
variable, and Maya had heard it come and go depending on the topic
of conversation or the listener. When he really wanted to win an
argument, he was certainly a Cuban. *It is not that simple*, he said,
putting a dead stop to the argument as to whether Kafka had fore-
seen something. He didn't seem to care for the argument whatsoever, but simply understood his power to intimidate. How could
they argue about totalitarianism, those fools, the ignorant? It is not
that simple, was all he had to say. He was one of the brighter students Maya had had. She considered him a true rarity. In the first
place, because he was exceedingly proud of his intellect; secondly,
because he was sexy. He was both contemplative and a bit of a
predator.

Maya desired him for many reasons. He was desirable. He was
forbidden as a youth and a Cuban. Cuba awed her—as a cultivated
mind among third world nations, as a place America feared and
hated. She felt he would know something she didn't. He would be
beautifully cynical. Together, they would cackle drunkenly and
close to sorrow. And not the least of her reasons—she knew that
he preferred white women, had seen and noted as much, and that
he would make an exception in her case because she was a professor. For this reason she was angry with him and would feel no guilt.
She felt she could overwhelm, devastate, control such a youth.

This part of her desire, Maya would not put name to. As young
as he was, she felt she had a right to him.

So here we are, the story at hand. Antonio knocked softly. Maya was not sure she heard it, so she continued to sit at her desk playing with the hem of her slacks. He knocked softly again. She said hello. The door did not open so she got up to open it. He stood there a good foot taller than she, and spoke his greeting in a voice just above a whisper. All that was audible was resonance.

Immediately, the good doctor felt she was deliciously defying taboo. He was not in her class that term. He had been in her class the previous term. As if a passing form might know and report this, report that a student was coming to see her in the *wrong semester*, Maya stuck her head out in the hall to make sure the coast was clear. She shut the door behind him. She gestured toward the seats.

Maya's spine curved, she held the corners of her desk, arms straightened, as if to keep it in place, as if in for tremors. Antonio spoke so quietly that she had to lean in a bit to hear him.

He used her title—"Dr. Capistrano," he said, and seemed to be choking a giggle. He asked how she was.

"Fine," Maya answered. She gathered herself. She leaned back and crossed her legs. Then her spine curved the other way. She contracted. They conversed—what are you studying this semester, how was your break, etc. And each time it was her turn to speak, Maya paused and caught her breath and her eyes became the slightest bit scrutinizing. She would appear disturbed and hesitant. She would appear to question his intentions.

It was understood that she must make a show of resistance. She would act a bit shocked at the idea. Everything about the meeting would be a show of decision making. The whole damn thing, spelled out already, should appear against her better judgment. She need only place her pauses carefully. When he left, there would be doubt and no doubt.

Ah, but some information has been withheld for purposes of narrative tension. Maya might have the desire to blame this on her former student. It would certainly look better before the omnipresent judge and jury, if the whole thing had been at his initiative, if she had argued, as the mature adult, against the idea. It all depends on where we start to hear the story. We could have started earlier. We could have begun that morning on the staircase, as Maya was climbing in her smart pants suit, her girlish hair down, her slight lateral movement. Between the secretary who didn't recognize her and the fourth-floor door to her department, she ran into the young man. Antonio was descending, she, ascending, and after smiling a new kind of smile as she passed, she turned back and gave him what is known as the once-over, the soulful eye. He started with surprise.

And here he was twenty-five minutes later. On the verge of laughter with nervousness, yet behaving in a directed way. She preened in his direction, purporting indifference, and sent him away. It was understood he should come back. He waited longer than expected—his show of resistance. She had several weeks to mull it over. She began to wonder if he'd lost his interest or nerve or if she'd shown too much supposed indifference. There was doubt and no doubt.

I T

Our greatest humiliations are things we bring upon ourselves. I do not mean our greatest sorrows or mournings. Certainly we suffer the most when we regret the way we loved and know we have no more opportunity to bestow a better love upon the beloved. This might be grief, with its own regrets, but it is not necessarily humiliation. Humiliation implies a greater audience and a specific sort of pain.

And perhaps we can forgive ourselves when a girl in gym class yanks down our shorts. We should have seen her coming, we might feel for a moment, but it won't really be our fault. And isn't her attention some form of compliment? But why, once in a great while, do we walk to the center of the room and expose our own disfigured panties?

We will stray now, a moment, from the story at hand, as Maya herself did.

About day ten, no word from the young man, Maya began to become very angry with herself for having desired Antonio in the first place. She had devoted much of her imagination to a sexual life with him. She had recalled, in exquisite detail, that his lower lip was a distinctly different shade from the upper. She had imagined them slightly parted and then hungry and aggressive. She had elaborated scenarios, all of which pointed to her attempt at resistance and his responsibility. Okay—just coffee, she would say the first time. It would have to be coffee on her back stoop where no one would see. Their lovemaking would have the nervous torturous build-up of a teenage tryst and yet be more fulfilling. Eventually—they'd drive to the city, where a couple such as they would turn heads only for the right reasons. They'd experience euphoric days of freedom.

She had allowed herself, a couple of times, a notion of permanence. A vision here or there of how he could support himself in the future. She had told X, of course, but not Y.

"I know you're gonna do it," X laughed. Dr. C sensed that X was infinitely relieved that C finally had an affair to speak of. "Teach him well," X said, and they spent some amount of time condescending to his youth and celebrating their own sexual prowess. They entered into conspiracy and C felt a surging affection for X, her only true friend in the world.

And now here it was, day ten, and no sign of life from Antonio. Dr. C had worn her best every day, including her better brassieres, and checked her office mailbox for notes. She had arranged herself in her desk chair. Her heart lifted when there was a knock at the door when the phone rang when the buzzer at home, etc., etc., etc. One day she thought she recognized, etc., etc., and it turned out to be a woman.

But this is not what is meant by the humiliation we bring upon ourselves. Yes, she was angry with herself about Antonio, about having expected so much of this, but what she did then was reach for a lamp to steady herself.

She awoke, day eleven, as tender as a bruise. Meaning, the form of her long-term depression mutated. Instead of a slight distaste, a slightly poisoned feel, or the illusion of an upward swing, or even her usual cantankerousness, Maya awoke feeling something like vulnerability. Vulnerability might not be the best word, because it implies primarily the potential for victim-hood. A better word would include just as well the possibility for joy. I will suggest tenuousness, which is also not quite right. Maya was just as close to euphoria as she was that dark familiar place. What she felt was subject to outside forces, to the wind. She was standing on the head of a pin and could fall in an infinite array of emotional directions, none of them her own choosing. She did not want them to be of her own choosing. She relinquished responsibility. She stood precariously and waited. She was very swollen and tender.

It was a Saturday. She went to the park. The wooden slats of the bench were at first too cold and then warmed to her body. She tucked her knees to her chin. Her black hair lifted in strands in the breeze.

She watched a young couple. They were sitting on the bench next to her, so Maya had to turn her head. There was no hiding her staring, but the kids were oblivious. The girl had a sweet chubby face, pale and flushing. The boy had a poor excuse for a mustache. He was rubbing her temples with two long slender fingers on each side. Her eyes were closed. She was sinking into the sensation. And then they stopped and pressed foreheads, and they spoke and laughed and then she lightly slapped him. The boy did not like this. He looked off. His jaw was set and an expression of terrible hurt came over his face.

This was when Maya noticed how moved she herself was, and yet she did not feel this was *it*. She felt there was an impending *it* for this day. That her surging emotions would somehow, at some point, have a feeling of completion, a specific direction and a completion. All she had to do was wait for the wind.

There were others to watch. She saw the mother holding herself together for the little girl's sake. The mother who had brought the little girl to play, who threw the nerf ball out and then out again. If one were watching closely, one could see that the mother's face had two layers. The top layer was an attempt at a smile. The underneath was a containment. Maya felt, in this moment, that mother-hood was very cruel. This too moved her in the same way—a compression in the chest as close to joy as misery. She noted that she had spent moments out of her own consciousness, congratu-lated herself on the escape and her own empathy.

It was soon thereafter that her tenderness became physical. Up until that moment it had been an emotional, almost cerebral, sensa-tion—one of observation and then reaction. And then her skin took on a feverishness. She pressed on her forearm expecting white spots to appear as they do after sunburn. She put her fingers in her mouth and thought it was an amazing sensation. She wanted hard candy. Her scalp was stretched tightly and wanted relief. She wanted to be stroked at the temples, felt she could faint of it.

For the first time in many a moon she had an overwhelming craving for a cigarette. She approached strangers, another young couple, disheveled, smoking, talking—probably students at the college—and asked for one. It was a good dizzying cigarette, and when she stood, she fell a bit to one side.

She lamented that she was in this sensual state and did not have Antonio.

Soon, deep in the downward spiral, she would reach for the lamp. She would mistake an idea for a good idea. This was not the same thing as the humiliation she brought upon herself. She could have forgiven herself for this particular lamp in and of itself.

She was hungry. She went to a Middle Eastern restaurant. It was an odd time to eat by then, late afternoon, and so she was the only one in the tiny place. There were five or six empty tables including the little one she took by the window. The proprietor said hello. She assumed he was the proprietor—it seemed a place this small would have to be owned and run by the same people.

Because the place was empty he said hello from across the room, from a corner near a display case of baked goods and the cash register. He was a big man, heavy set, wearing a white shirt which strained a bit at the buttons. He had balded so that his hairline made a V-shape into his forehead. His face was wide and flat and pointed severely at the nose and the chin, as if someone had pressed these two features toward each other. He was nearly twenty years older than our dear heroine.

There she was at her table for one by the window, flesh raised with goosebumps, waiting for *it*. She sat up straight and put her napkin in her lap, suddenly more ladylike than was her usual inclination. She flipped through the menu, closed it, and waited for the proprietor's approach. She ordered in a shy girl's voice and then crossed her legs, one pointed foot bouncing over the other.

She had decided something about this middle-aged man. She

had decided that he was infinitely embraceable. That soft flesh was nice, that he would have a more generous spirit than anyone she had recently known. That he was one of the few people in the world she would not have to protect herself against. She had an overwhelming urge to be folded into him, that this was *it*. Her mouth fell open with relief. She would be comforted.

So what she did was, she waited until he was looking away and then she stared, averting her eyes quickly when he caught her. Maya had to perform this operation a few times before it seemed to register. The proprietor, with his wide flat face and his sweeping gesture, he was scooping up falafel and dropping it in the fry basket. It had been many a year since the man had experienced this sort of interest from a young woman. And then—his lips parted into an amazed smile, a wet open smile like the mouth of a clown.

"So you like falafel…?" he asked grinning, staring and nodding, staring and nodding.

"Yes, I like falafel," said our darling heroine, with her little foot bouncing.

He gave her the lunch on the house. She set up a rendezvous at her place. He brought wine.

And of course, by the time he arrived several hours later, by the time he had shut up the little place and pulled the iron gate down to the sidewalk and locked it, she had completely lost her desire. Her skin was no longer feverish. The tenderness had waned to normalcy.

By the time he arrived she was good and disgusted with herself but didn't know how to unravel so she decided to go on with it, get it over with as quickly as possible. She kissed him passionately as he entered and then avoided kissing him as much as possible. She gulped wine. She made sure the lights were completely off, allowed things to be *done* to her. She hated the way he continually licked her face. She felt his hair where it was oiled, smelled pomade. She felt his chest soft and jiggling against her own, his stomach, flattening, spreading, widening. Then she sent him, thank god, home to his wife.

She sat on the edge of her bed for a time with her shoulders pinched up around her ears and her nostrils flared. Then she went to the liquor store and got herself drunk. She didn't even tell X.

OKAY—NOW, WHAT SHE *REALLY* BROUGHT UPON HERSELF

As do most of us, dear sweet Maya had a few periods of her life which she used as controls by which to measure everything else. That which is not equal to one of the three extended periods of euphoria, is not truly her life, but in-between time. Everything is and has been the in-between time except for 1) the time she and X, as teenagers, worked at Owen's Pizza and discovered that there were men in the world who admired them; 2) the summer of her college boyfriend; 3) when she was mid-novel and post-dissertation, had recently received an appointment, and was running about the city with Madam Y, who was just finishing her own novel. They were reveling in their brilliance, charm and good looks. Maya had had lovers. She was pure impending glory.

This was certainly not her life, this standing before her Russian Literature class, back turned, chalk raised (paper #3: Dostoyevski), with those horrible young eyes, the righteous, scrutinizing eyes of youth burrowing into her back. Our young professor was awash with shame and it would only get worse.

She lectured that day with a quiver in her voice, off toward a corner. This was two days after picking up the falafel proprietor. The day before she had spent in the cloud of hangover. That was easier.

Now she had to live with herself.

They were bored and bold, her students, yawning toward the ceiling, looking at their watches, openly sneering—oh, even with her back turned Maya could sense their judgment. Their open acknowledgment of her failure. The young women poised on their little butts, and the guys—they were worse—with their arms folded and their knees spread to a stance of hostility.

She was particularly conscious of two of them. Marguerite was a Russian girl who sat in front and took careful notes. She had soft glowing skin, a pimple here or there, and cascading blond ringlets. She had a quality of unbroken concentration, and if Maya were to fuck anything up—misunderstand a principle of Russian culture, say, or get a date wrong—oh, Marguerite with her relentless stare, she would be the one to catch her.

The other student who made her particularly nervous had already, at one point, caught her. Dr. C refered to him in her pretty, pained, little head as "the Senator's Son." He had a famous last name, though she couldn't be certain. He certainly had the educational background of a senator's son—was a freshman in a 300-level course and regularly quoted Nietzsche and Jung. He had breeding, a right of inheritance. She envied his security. At nineteen, he had already read what she had achieved perhaps half way through her graduate studies.

And one day, on a sick hairpin turn of the downward spiral, he had caught her fucking up. She had wanted to make a point about idealism and so had quickly drawn Plato's Cave on the board. First of all, she did not remember the configuration of the cave, and second of all, did not remember what shapes made the shadows and so drew a cow. Then, she drew the source of light, a bonfire, coming from the wrong direction, so that logically, there should have been no shadows at all. A section of the class snickered, but it was the Senator's Son who spoke up audibly.

"There is a long passageway going down," he said snidely, "and it's puppets." Maya's face reddened, etc., etc. She ignored him and carried defensively on. Since then she had avoided the young man, although she was quite relieved when his first paper was late and wracked with spelling errors, and though it was well executed in every other way, she got to mark it up considerably and give him a C+.

All this is beside the point. Where we are now is with Maya two days after she reached for a big fat ol' lamp. Her back is to the classroom, her chalk raised and she feels the eyes of Marguerite, the much-smarter-than-her young Russian, and the Senator's Son. She feels them burning with teen-age rancor and she hears their disrespectful sighs. Who put her in charge anyway? She stood there with her chalk and walked through bad-teaching memories that made her wince; then she thought of the old man's face when he was fucking her—she had tried not to look at him but she did, at one point, catch sight of brown gums, pink extended tongue, and an expression of unbearable gratitude.

Somebody cleared a throat. Maya had no idea how long she'd been standing in the same position. She went on to finish class in the same way, going from a whiny girl's voice to long moments of distraction. When class was over, the usual handful of students stayed after to ask questions, and each one approaching, each long youthful stride, Maya felt was someone coming to accuse her of something: not making sense, not knowing what she was talking about—asking her, perhaps, where she got her B.A.—which wouldn't be good enough, which should have been somewhere else ...*Can I hand in my paper on Friday will you be in your office hours tomorrow I was thinking about discussing the use of etc. etc.*

She waited until everyone was gone in order to avoid unnecessary small talk. And then when she turned to walk out the door, horror of horrors, there was Chandran smiling and waving hello.

Maya froze. She glanced about for an escape. She could not possibly face Chandran in this condition.

What a striking woman Dr. Ch was with those curvy Indian eyes, that incredible black hair, just exactly the person who should have been Maya's new best friend, a smart and striking woman, and here was C, buckling, caving, cringing. Maya hunched over her briefcase as if it were falling. As if it could protect her.

Dr. Ch waited in the doorway while Maya stood still, longer than was socially acceptable. Confusion crossed Chandran's face. Maya stood immobile in the center of the classroom.

"Will you be in the office?" Ch finally asked.

Maya nodded and exhaled with relief as Chandran walked away. Then she darted off campus, started to head home and felt like asshole enough that she stopped, turned right around and went back to the Comp Lit Department.

Maya paced in her office, bracing herself. Her fingers wormed excitedly about at her sides. Okay, all she had to do was make a few moments of small talk with Chandran. Maya concentrated on small talk. Where are you from? How do you like the department? I am from ThisPlace, Midwest, USA. My parents are from the Philippines. No, I have never been there. Yes, I want very much to see it. Okay, she was ready. But for a slight feeling of nausea and an uncontrollable curling and uncurling of the fingers, she was ready.

When Maya heard the approach of footsteps, she had a last rush of panic over her outfit (my god when will I start dressing like a grown woman, look at the loudness of these colors, did my pants have to be flared like the *students* are wearing?), but successfully opened the door and greeted the lovely Ms. Chandran. "Call me, Anita."

Dr. C successfully made the smallest of talk. How was lecture today? Dr. Ch confessed to having had a bad one while C only said, "Fine," and nodded quickly.

After a moment, Maya noticed that she was blocking the door-way. That she had not invited Anita in, but had stood with one elbow against one side of the opening and an extended arm toward the other, as if there were a terrible secret inside. Maya noticed this gaffe, but then felt she was too late to rectify it, so only shifted her stance to try and make it appear less uptight. Then after another moment, Maya noticed that it was her turn to speak, so she opened her mouth. She groped for a question. Um, uh.

She took so long that Anita saved her. "Would you like to join me for a coffee? I was going to the Café Café…isn't that adorable?"

Coffee? The question. *Coffee.* The answer. And though some-thing deep in her bowels warned Dr. Maya that this would be excru-ciating, she said yes, and the two walked off side by side. En route, Maya was able to rely on the earlier rehearsal in her office. Dr. Ch was from Bombay, had done undergraduate work at Cambridge (this brought a burning sensation to the place where Maya's spine met her skull) and graduate work at Yale. Maya mentioned only her graduate school.

They arrived. They waited awkwardly in line. Maya shifted her weight and rolled her eyes up toward the ceiling, concentrating. "Um, how do you like the department?" she asked, but then did not hear the answer because she was absorbed in keeping her lunch down. Maya felt wretched. Two days before, she had allowed a com-plete stranger to sweat over her for no reason at all but that she had had a hot flash in the afternoon. The greatest sin, however, was that he was old and saggy, and roamed freely about the little college town out in the middle of nowhere. He could have walked into that coffee shop just then, for example, as Anita was sizing her up.

When Maya's turn came, a kid, who looked vaguely familiar, had to remove one half his blaring headphones to nudge her. She ordered cappuccino and the two young doctors balanced their hot mugs to the condiment table and then balanced them over to a perfectly lovely little table by the window.

Chandran drank tea, dunking and floating her tea bag, dunking and floating. They sat between a poet on one side, a bearded young man looking off soulfully over his notebook, and a couple on the other. The couple, a young Asian woman, who also looked vaguely familiar, and a young white gentleman, were whispering quickly. They sat next to each other facing the center of the establishment as if this were a cabaret with a floor show.

Chandran was clearing her throat in a light feminine way. Capistrano felt her musculature kinking—somewhere something had been jammed into the wrong place and misaligned everything else. One moment a nerve in her neck configured into a small hard rock, and then it was the curve along the top of her foot, her calf.

"And so how are you getting on this semester?" Ch asked. Maya felt herself blush. She thought of Plato's cave. She struggled to answer, but then was saved by an employee who came over and lifted their steaming mugs with one hand, sprayed a solution on the table, and wiped with the other. The two professors crinkled their button noses.

"Goes well with my tea," Chandran said, in the same light feminine voice. Capistrano laughed awkwardly. Silence ensued. Capistrano remembered the question. How was she getting on. She did remember that it was her turn to speak but was overwhelmed by the infinite possibilities of her answer. Should she tell Chandran how fucked up she was? Should she tell her about the Senator's Son and his burrowing eyes? If there were anyone within a two-hundred-mile radius who might be the one to speak to, Chandran was she.

Maya parted her lips to speak and then changed her mind. She lifted a straw full of whipped cream off of her cappuccino. The cream fell, landing in her lap. She tried to clean up the mess with a napkin but only succeeded in spreading the white stain so that it covered a good portion of her upper thigh.

Maya was profoundly aware of her own ineptitude and felt

her eyes beginning to water. She bit her lower lip.

But then. But then, the most amazing thing happened. Dr. C looked up, glanced over at her companion and saw in Dr. Ch's face concern, if not empathy.

A wave of relief washed over our first good doctor, a delicious cousin to vertigo. Every knot in her body suddenly gave way. She had coiled and twisted and then burst free. With it came exhaustion. She had been wired with tension and the slightest touch of sincere affection had erased this tension and now she was ready to collapse. She saw white spots. She had trouble staying awake. She had to fight to remember where she was, to listen to what Chandran was saying.

"Are you all right?" Chandran asked. And Capistrano said that yes, she was all right and meant it. "I'm just suddenly very, very tired."

Maya was too weary to notice how long they sat without saying anything. Anita simply took up the ball and began telling a story.

"You know when one begins using the lecturer's voice in the completely inappropriate place?"

Yes, Maya said. *Yes, I understand.* And Maya with her eyes open and a stain of cream in her lap, it could be said that she fell asleep right there, that for a moment she lost consciousness, was unaware of where she was, and when she woke up, Chandran was in another place in the story

"...and it was quite embarrassing, actually. I found myself projecting toward the far reaches of the establishment..."

"You think that's bad," Maya interrupted, with impish enthusiasm, with a hurried tone of intimacy, "the other day I had a one-night stand with this complete stranger. He had a belly like this." She threw a hand over her gut and shook it, imitating a jello-like consistency.

Chandran set her ear forward as if she were not quite sure she had heard correctly. She seemed about to ask a question and then thought again and sat back, looking at Maya with clear intense discomfort.

There it was. She had done it. She had walked to the center of the gym, looked for the infamous girl who yanked down shorts, and not finding her, had volunteered to go on alone.

The entire surface area of Capistrano's body flashed cold and then hot. This was worse than having fucked the old man in the first place. This was worse than Plato's Cave. This would make it entirely impossible to ever face Chandran again. Maya was consumed by hot waves. She began to shake and then her mouth grimaced. Anita was searching the corners of the room as if they would provide the graceful escape plan.

It was Ch who politely excused herself after prolonged silence. Maya said, "Take care of yourself," gritting her teeth, remaining in her seat.

II

COMFORT

Maya told herself twice. If he comes now, I won't. It has been too long. If he comes now, I won't. Perhaps if she had told herself once, it would have worked. But she told herself twice.

Two major goals remained for Capistrano. These were that she was to avoid Chandran at all costs and resist Antonio should the need arise.

On the first day, miracle of miracles, she awoke feeling quite *shrewd*. That is, she awoke feeling a preciseness to her concentration, a definiteness to her decisions, which had been absent for quite some time. Her ridiculousness came clear, and though she knew she was not ready to abandon her ridiculousness (and make peace, for example, with Ch), she felt she understood it and was ready, even, to forgive herself for this somewhat. *This too shall pass.* She thought, and knew that in time her mind would be free of these strange forces. She must only hold herself together until her confidence returned, until she was back to her old self. She made plans for the future. She conceived of a second, superior novel, and the school in the city which would hire her so she could return there too. Yes, in the city there were people like her. She would not be dependent on *one* colleague for friendship and a boy for romance.

This clarity lasted well into the afternoon at which time, as if someone had turned her a notch up, played the LP on the wrong speed, adrenaline burst into her veins and brought with it the shakes—a tight impossible thought loop and a physical impreciseness. She decided to visit Chandran and explain her embarrassment. She decided to visit Chandran and pretend as if nothing had happened. She imagined bopping Chandran one. She thought of explaining her embarrassment. And each time she made a decision, Maya felt a bit of panic that it was the wrong decision, a constriction of the ribs about the heart. She would decide to wait until she could concentrate, but the question would arise again against her will.

She did things quickly. She ate as if someone would rip the plate out from under her, shoving mouthfuls in while the previous was only briefly chewed. She made drowning noises as she swallowed. She made lecture notes that were slashes and loops, incomprehensible even to her. She spilled her penholder, yanked out her drawer violently and then replaced it so that only one side was properly on the runners. She exhaled constantly, with her cheeks bloated and her lips pursed, as people do when they are trying to contain stress, when they are trying to concentrate. She thought that she would tell Antonio, if he came, that she would just, but then again she might, and if he were...

She darted from office to library to lecture hall, with her head down, as if, if she didn't *see* Chandran, the woman wouldn't exist.

Of course, that night, the tension would not let up and no amount of alcohol would put her to sleep. She lay on her bed until the sun rose, staring at the ceiling and dismantling previous decisions. By midday, day number two, she was blindingly weary.

She watched the world through a milky film and stared into space for long periods. A few times that day, she dreamed waking, thought she heard things—her name being called, a phone ringing subtly throughout the library. If, day one, we could characterize her lecture as jarring and disjointed (she leapt quickly from one subject to another, presented observations about particular pages without giving particular page numbers), then, day two, we might use the terms "dreamy" and "diffuse" (she trailed off into mumbles, responded to her students' commentary with an "uh-huh," not remembering anything they said).

She had a Chandran-sighting just before the end of the day, opened her office door to glimpse the linguist receding down the hall. Anita had a single paper in her hand which waved a bit as she stepped. Maya slipped back inside, quickly, quietly, and held the door knob until the pounding of her heart gave way.

Evening two, she fell immediately into the deepest part of sleep, dreamed vividly as we usually do closer to morning. She dreamed she was an idiot infant left out on the ice to die and darted awake to vague sounds. It was an hour after she had lain down. These were vague sounds such as we hear echoing when we're weary. As she'd heard phones and her name earlier in the day. *Mirages* of sound. I do not say hallucinations because under hallucinations we fear for our sanity. Mirages we understand—they are visitations brought by extremes; we forgive ourselves for them. We were thirsty and crawling through the desert. We were in mourning and saw ghosts of our beloved. Maya awoke to an audial mirage—so she was aware of an old woman howling. She was frightened, but not for her sanity. She was deathly afraid of being *alone*.

This was the howling old woman's terror as well.

She grew particularly conscious of the space beneath her bed, of what it had the room to hide. Maya sat up. Her mind raced everywhere for comfort and the only thing which came to her, the only sensual image which could overpower the groanings of loneliness, was herself in Antonio's arms.

On some level, she knew this was silly, but it worked. It was like the fits of terror she would experience in strange houses, baby-sitting as an adolescent. The thought of the children sleeping in the next room somehow made it easier to face the forces of serial killers or the supernatural which combed the streets searching for the likes of her. Yes, the children were completely dependent on her for the very most basic functions of their bodies, and yet, this dependency comforted her.

Antonio was a generation behind her, a generation and a half, perhaps, if one measures them in terms of lingo, pop culture, style. How could she expect some sort of paternal protection and comfort? But she did, and the idea of laying in his arms stayed her fear. The howling faded.

THE APPLE REJECTED

Day three, she was teaching. It wasn't so bad today. The lecture was even, approaching, not all that close, but approaching, let's say, a good day. She jiggled the chalk in her hand in the manner of a professor. She said, "I'd like to call your attention to…" She cleared her throat and made a profound observation and then said, "…moving on…" She traced her finger through the text and made another profound observation. She heard their papers rustling, their pens. She felt somewhere in the realm of competence. She was a dancer, posture impeccable, bending knees to prepare for elevation onto that false toe, and then, that dumbshit, she made the mistake of looking straight back at the Senator's Son.

The Senator's Son was bent over, looking at the bottom of his shoe, quite consumed by this activity. His face had that hateful smile. A cocked smile, one half of the mouth pulled back and prepared. He chewed gum so that the gum was visible. He was big and poured himself over the chair.

Maya felt a rush of fury. She made efforts to contain herself. She finished the lecture, after a bit of an awkward pause, reddening. She began discussion. The first question she asked was "So, what do you think?"

No reply. The Russian girl realigned her knees and a boy in the back with mid-length hair flipped his bangs back. She asked why Anna Karenina did something or other. She asked why Tolstoy chose a given method of relaying this something or other. Blank stares. A fourth question occurred to her.

"Honestly, has anyone read this?" she asked flatly, as if not in judgment, but for curiosity. This was a trick. This mood lasted fifteen seconds. During those fifteen seconds, Marguerite shyly raised her hand and the young Heir Apparent shifted his gum to the other cheek. When the fifteen seconds were up Dr. C was enraged. Nobody had read the work and that big little fucker in back was maligning her personally with his body language. She imagined her usual act of violence, but had to add an element of surprise, as the young man was obviously twice her size, and quite possibly much more remorseless. She was forced to imagine stealing up on him, catching him unawares from behind.

"Okay, okay," she barked, shuffling papers, without looking up. "Then we'll just have to have a little quiz." The students looked one to the other. They had never had a quiz before. Some sat up more. Some opened their mouths in a dumb surprised expression.

"Come on now," she said, looking off into a corner of the floor "take out some paper." They slowly prepared themselves with pen and paper and then the good doctor stood there for some time with her finger on her chin thinking up a question. She announced the question just as the allotted hour for class was ending. Several students gathered their books and left without handing in anything. The rest wrote something quickly and hustled their loose leaf papers to the front of the class. Only Marguerite sat thoughtfully and then wrote out a full paragraph.

Maya shuffled through the quote-unquote quizzes as the classroom emptied out. Only Marguerite gave a legitimate answer. A handful apologized. I'm sorry I wasn't able to, etc. Some simply wrote their names on the paper, and a few wrote phrases obviously edged with deep hostility. "I never knew we would be being quizzed, so…" Dr. Capistrano balled up the Heir Apparent's and threw it out without looking, so frightened was she of his response.

She stood there for quite some time, picking at the shreds on the sides of papers. She fought an urge to throw them all away, knowing she would never make record of the strange little exercise.

Antonio appeared in the doorway. He carried his books under his arm and Maya observed immediately that his face was smooth and beautiful and that he needed a haircut.

He was nervous. His eyes widened doe-ishly and he seemed rooted in the door frame. Seeing him this way took our good doctor's mind off of her own ineptitude. She beckoned him in. He stood across the podium from her. There was a moment in which Maya felt squeamish watching him, he was so wracked with nerves. He was pinching up behind the neck like a kitten, as if an outside force had control. He made a few false starts with whatever it was he had to say. This did not correspond with her sexual fantasies.

Dr. C became aware of the open doors and the possibility that a student from the next class might come in and spot them standing together. It was not a normal student-teacher stance.

Antonio produced an apple. A huge, perfectly shaped, red, juicy specimen.

Maya did not have a bag with her. She had a small purse, a flat-ish briefcase, a clipboard, and a copy of *Anna Karenina*. She was sure that if she carried that apple across the yard toward her office, it would be obvious that it was a gesture of courtship from a student from the wrong semester, whom she had encouraged in a *sexual manner*. If she took the apple, Chandran herself would catch Capistrano, and Maya would stand there stuttering, explaining its presence.

"I can't take that," she said accusingly.

"You don't like it?" Antonio asked. He turned stiffly with sur-prise. He looked from one direction to the other without the use of his neck, as if he wore a brace. His voice was low and intimate.

Two things bothered Maya. One, that it had taken him two weeks to get to this moment (the coward, she thought). Two, that he did not seem to understand the magnitude of their proposed affair, what she had at risk. Couldn't he have found a less public way to approach her? A note in the mailbox? A phone call?

She feared that he was doing this *for* public knowledge. Wouldn't their affair elevate him, just as it would denigrate her in the eyes of her colleagues? Would he not be an even sexier figure on campus if he had an affair with Maya? Would she not be an even more untrusted, in fact, *ridiculous* figure (a child who could not han-dle the responsibility)? She already felt like the bad daughter of the office, and here he was broadcasting it all over the little reasonably-respected-but-not-outstanding college out in the middle of nowhere. She couldn't believe his selfishness. The nerve.

She threw up her hands before the apple. She glared at him. She, in effect, ousted him. She stood still with her hands in the air. His eyes darted over her face and then, as if carried by the loose skin of his neck, as if not of his own volition, he stumbled recklessly, jar-ringly, out of the classroom door.

RITUAL AND THE UNKNOWN

It did not take Maya very long to realize what she had done. A pro-found loneliness descended upon her. She turned to Madam X, who moaned with exasperation into the phone and told her to fix it. C knew that she would have to make a move if it were ever going to happen. This did not coincide with her reasoning that it should appear as if he had seduced her. Now she would have to take responsibility, sin outright.

She tried to call him. She disguised her voice when she called campus information, just in case. She raised it an octave or two to best imitate a co-ed. She felt she was convincing.

He was not listed. Neither was he listed in the town's directory. She went shuffling through papers and found a dorm number on a roster. This would feel somehow more slimy, more illegal, than any other approach, so she took a few days to think about it.

In the meantime, Dr. C made the acquaintance of one Elaine or Ellen (she could never remember) Alstov, a sociology professor.

Maya had taken to bringing her lunch, of course, eating in her office for fear that any campus eatery would hold Chandran, and any off-campus place, Chandran and/or the Middle Eastern proprietor. She could never get up early enough to prepare herself something decent, so every day she brought herself a cup of instant noodles. Collecting the necessary hot water from the faculty lounge was always nerve-wracking.

One day, she absolutely positively had to have another flavor, and she decided that she would never find Ch in the Wendy's around the corner and up the street. She slunk out, head lowered.

She ordered a chicken salad with french dressing and settled in a little plastic chair near the trash bin. She faced the wall. She had been particularly attracted to the peas in her salad, and dug right in, scooping up a number of them. She had been anticipating the juicy pop between her teeth, but was disappointed to find they created only a powdery deflating sensation.

Behind her someone was playing their headphones at the highest possible volume. The type of music was unidentifiable. It was a massive buzzing, like locusts descending, and it gave Maya the creeps.

She turned around and sneered at the kid, who looked vaguely familiar, but he was too absorbed in the rhythms to make note of her wrath.

A woman came and sat at the table next to her, which was unusual. There were many empty seats in the place, and few opt, as did our darling heroine, to sit facing the wall, close to the trash.

Maya bent further over her salad, gathered her elbows around it. She had not yet glanced at the woman, but felt herself being watched.

The woman had a fit of coughs. The first few coughs sounded surface-y—as one might signal a discomfort in conversation or simply in response to a scratch in the throat. Then they took on a deep liquid resonance. They went on for some time.

Finally, Maya looked over. One of the most petite women she had ever seen in her life was sitting next to her. She was lost in her orange plastic seat like a child, and every detail of her bones was visible. The woman had brown hair, creased in back as if it had just been released from a barrette, and a lock at the top of the skull which bunched up the way hair does for the just-woken.

"Are you okay?" Maya asked. "Do you want some water?"

The woman nodded and continued coughing into her fist. Her entire body shook as if she would bounce out of her seat. Maya went to the counter and got some water for the woman. After a sip or two, the coughing subsided.

Maya did not want to further engage in conversation and dug back into her salad with her head down. She turned away a bit, afraid to catch something. When she was chasing her last chunk of chicken around the plastic container with her spork, the kid behind her somehow found more volume on his Walkman and it became like sitting over a subway line. Maya had an irresistable urge to share this observation with somebody and looked to the woman she had been avoiding. When she glanced over, the woman already had her eyes on Maya, had turned her body toward her.

The thin woman was eating a shake. Wendy's shakes are nearly as thick as ice cream, so that the woman was able to eat only from the center of her cup, leaving a tunnel and forming a tube-shaped wall of shake.

"It's like sitting over a subway," Maya said, gesturing toward the kid. The woman nodded vigorously and then offerered her hand.

"Ellen Alstov," she said, or Elaine.

"Maya." She felt, somehow, that keeping her last name from this woman would keep her safe.

"Do you teach at the school?"

Maya was actually taken aback by the question, a bit insulted. No one had ever assumed she was anything but a student before. She wondered if she were aging rapidly. She nodded. "How did you know?"

Ellen pointed to a smear of chalk which ran diagonally from Maya's right thigh to her bellybutton. Then she was consumed by another fit of coughing which began lightly and built and eventually subsided. Maya sat still for a while. The hacking had given her goose bumps. It felt like something lawless.

The silence went on for too long.

"And you?" Maya asked. The woman, Elaine, nodded.

"What do you teach?"

Maya explained herself and then reciprocated with the same question.

"I'm in the Sociology Department."

They continued with small talk. Between every exchange, Maya was tempted to let the conversation lapse, and then after that extra beat, she would continue it anyway. "What courses are you teaching this semester?"

Ellen stuck the wrong end of her spork into what was left of her shake.

"Social Deviance," she said. Maya looked down. A file lay on the table between them. It was labeled with large black letters— "DEVIANCE"

"How interesting."

Alstov smiled humbly. "Right now, I'm teaching an essay about ritual." She went on to explain that the more chance there is involved in an undertaking, the more ritual the practitioners engage in. She used baseball as an example. "Fielders tend to rely on things which have worked in the past—lucky hats, large pancake breakfasts. But pitchers, they think that's a load of crap…" She lit a cigarette, and after a moment of inhaling, began to ash into the hole in her shake. She went on, "Societies which are subject to catastrophic weather tend to be more ritualistic…"

"Excuse me," came an adolescent voice, unidentifiable immediately as male or female. Maya and Elaine looked up to find a teenage girl, a Black girl with a long collection of braids, spray-bottle in hand, standing above them in the Wendy's uniform. "You can't smoke that in here."

Alstov inhaled once more to signal her rebellion, and then, sneering, dropped what was left of her cigarette in the center of what was left of her shake. It made a liquid hiss as it extinguished. She glared at the girl, her tongue pushing up her cheek a bit, nodding, as if making note of this infraction. The girl glared back.

"Well," Maya said, standing. "Better get back…"

Ellen whipped her jacket off of her chair and stood in one swift motion. She kept her cutting eyes on the girl until they were half way out of the establishment, like a dancer who turns the head last of all.

Maya was again surprised by how small her companion was. Dr. C was short herself, 5′2″ to be exact, and Dr. A was at least a few inches shorter. It was difficult to judge, as Ellen had an unusual way of walking. With each step, she rose up onto the full extension of her feet and then fell to a squat. She seemed to be riding a wheel which raised and lifted her with each rotation.

Elaine muttered angrily.

"So, um, ritual increases with chance." Maya brought this up both to distract the learned sociologist from her contemplation of the incident and because the concept fascinated her.

"Yes, with the unknown." Dr. Alstov said this with one last long hard look at Wendy's. She said these words with all of her concentrated rancor, like a rehearsed line, clearly having nothing to do with what she was actually thinking.

"Ritual and the unknown. Yes, we pray in times of need, don't we?"

"And turn to psychics."

"Yes, psychics and tarot readers and therapists."

Alstov seemed to return to the present. She went on to tell a story. She said that when she was in college she had a rough year. She said that those were the best years of other people's lives but not hers. Not only did she have family problems, and she said this wincing, waving it all away, but she had medical problems, terrible pains in her gut a doctor couldn't explain. She had seen three. She called a medical psychic.

"Now," Elaine said, "I believe there are millions of fakes out there. I mean, I tried the Psychic Friends Network. What a load of crap." They came to a corner and paused, waiting for traffic to clear. Alstov coughed lightly and put her hand to Maya's arm to steady herself. "But there are—and I know this for a fact—a handful of people out there who can really see the future."

Maya considered this. A chill ran up her spine.

"So I called this medical psychic. I asked him, what is this, when will this suffering end? He said—they'll remove your left ovary in June. Sure enough, I told the doctors to look into my ovaries—no one had thought of it." Alstov dug into her purse for her pack of Carltons. She lit one, bent down, cupping the flame in the wind. "All my problems fell away." The cigarette bobbed in her mouth as she spoke.

They came to the final intersection before campus and paused, watching the traffic. Maya felt relieved. She felt she had been given permission by an intellectual to turn to forces larger than herself. That someonesomething might hold her hand into the unknown. It was acceptable to feel this way. She could ask the heavens when she would recover, when fate would bring her something good. The light changed. They crossed the street, and Dr. Alstov promised to come by and collect Dr. Capistrano for another lunch one day.

Maya finished her day feeling liked. She turned the possibilities of ritual against the unknown over in her brain. She considered therapy, which she had been fundamentally against. Felt Freud was as delicious a fiction as anything. That turning to the system of psy-chotherapy was the same as turning to the Bible. But, *ya know*, she had been in pain and she was beginning to understand the need for such systems—the Bible, Freud, the Socialist Revolution. Something greater than oneself. Love, even. She wanted to surrender herself. It

was okay to want to surrender. It was a natural part of our makeup.
Alstov had done so. There was a reason humanity had always done
so.

Ritual and the unknown. She felt particularly proud of what she
was obsessing on. Her mind was not a little nodule, a little hard ker-
nel of self-hatred, of shame. She was not hoping for a knight in shining armor. She would have an abstract idea to discuss with her dear
smart friend Madam Y. She would have an impressive way of thinking. C was lucky enough to find Y at home and they had a wonderful
enthusiastic discussion about Alstov (Maya descibed her so vividly,
howling with delight as she parodied the hateful cigarette episode),
baseball positions and ritual, therapy, psychics and tarot cards.

This is what Y said, and it was beautiful, and Maya took it with
her. "It is like when you flip a coin to decide between movies. If the
coin lands on tails, and tails is the film you want to see just a bit
less, it might force you to realize what you truly want, or confirm a
decision you weren't even aware you had made. It's all like that. You
go to the system feeling you don't know, and it all makes you realize
what you do know."

"Yes," Maya said. "Yes." Y was so articulate on the subject that
C felt her dear friend must have been turning it over in her mind as
well.

Maya spent the evening in a hot bath considering all sorts of
plans. She could go into therapy. She could buy self-help books if
she wanted, ask Alstov for the number of that medical psychic. She
could read more psychoanalysis. The answer was there, *in her out
there*. It would be coming, if she went to meet it half way.

HER OWN MORAL UNIVERSE

She checked Buddhist chants out of the library. She fingered Gloria Steinem's self-help book in the bookstore. She waved at Chandran in the hallway, although it would be untrue to say she was anything but profoundly relieved when a student approached the linguist and left her unavailable. Yes, things would be different from here on out, boy. A new era was rising. She would create her own world, the future was in her hands, and because she was mapping out her own moral universe, it was certainly okay if she pulled out that old roster and looked up Antonio's dorm number.

She raised her voice an octave to disguise it. She was certain she sounded like a poor excuse for a transvestite and would relay the story to X using just that detail. X would enjoy that detail. A voice which was vaguely familiar answered and said Antonio did not live there anymore.

Maya tapped the eraser of her brand new perfectly sharpened pencil against her desk. She lay her pretty little head against her hand, plotting.

She had to watch for a few days. She had to stare out of her centrally located office window, watch the green lawn of the campus, the doors to the library (yes, everyone will eventually have to venture into the library). And then one day, there he was, lighting a cigarette by the founder's statue. It was perhaps not the best of opportunities. He was standing with two other students, one a tall thin blond young man in combat boots. Maya had had the tall thin young man in combat boots in her class. He was intelligent, an articulate writer, but every paper he wrote revealed his politics, and Dr. C considered him a bit of a Nazi. Just a touch. The other was a pretty young girl, a brunette, with pink plastic barrettes in her hair. She was tucked under the tall thin thing's arm. They were engaged in animated conversation. Antonio in particular would make his points with great fervor. At one point, he made a wide circle of disagreement, a good dozen steps, throwing up his hands and shaking his head.

They were smoking, so Capistrano knew that she had at least until the end of a cigarette to decide if this were the right opportunity. It would be very public. She would have to find the right excuse to get him alone. She approximated four to seven minutes.

She watched. She loved his gesturing. He was held loosely together, like a marionette. There seemed to be no tension in his body—his moves had tiny echoes, ripples. First he would shake his head dramatically from right to left, and then it would wobble a touch afterwards. He would shrug deeply, ears to shoulders, and then he would bounce a bit on his heels.

He inhaled deeply, and she could not see the length of the cigarette from where she sat, but because he was inhaling with that preciousness, the last bit, she burst down the stairs.

She was breathing a bit heavily. The two young men were talking. Only the girl noticed Maya before she spoke. "Excuse me, " Maya said. They were surprised and, it seemed, a bit appalled that she would stop them mid-sentence.

"Could I have a word with you?" Maya asked Antonio.

First she collected him beside the library doors and then, that being too public, she led him into the stacks of the library.

Throughout the whole interaction, he seemed about to burst into laughter. He carried a cocked expression, one on the verge of laughter. She said nothing at first. She gestured with her thumb and her pinkie and her fist, imitating a phone. He handed her his notebook. She went to write on the back of it, and that being too public, she flipped open the book and wrote on the last inside page. There was a drawing of a dinosaur there, with a huge, flame-like tail.

"When?" he mouthed.

"Tuesday," she said, and then she could see his nerves. She

could see his fear clearly apparent. He shuffled there with his feet wide apart, with his ass leaning up like a child in diapers. "What time?" he asked.

"Seven," and they separated.

He called on the following Sunday.

That Tuesday afternoon, she had been quite euphoric. Ellen/Elaine stopped by her office asking if she'd like to have dinner and Maya declined with a rain check. They chatted for a moment, and our darling heroine relayed the coin analogy. Yes, Alstov said, a finger to her chin, that is precisely it. Capistrano referred to her vaguely as "Elleine," as a compromise, and smiled warmly throughout the visit.

Who says your lover has to be your peer? Maya asked of the heavens when she arrived home. She was looking in the mirror, feeling quite attractive. She dropped her eyelids and puckered. She allowed herself a sexual fantasy. She allowed herself to sink into the idea of another. She had a lover. She had a lover.

After some time, she called Y and even told the story of Antonio. "Are you ever gonna change?" Y asked, and Maya felt the old friend was teasing her warmly. Emboldened, she called Chandran. There was some relief in the fact that she was not home, and Maya left a message inviting her out for Saturday afternoon.

"Perhaps we could attend the cinema," Maya said enticingly into the machine. Her pronunciation was somewhat like the linguist's own British inflection.

She went out for a walk at ten and when she got back there was still no word. She was angry, but confident he would still call, and decided to play it by ear. She drank a glass of water which tasted faintly of dust.

RECOGNITION

What she would eventually come to be amazed with would be how far she let it go. That she would allow herself to be hurt by a child, thirteen years younger than herself. That she would call back, with her disguised voice wavering, code name Zelda (he eventually informed her that his roommate was in her class), long after his anger and resistance had settled into indifference.

When she turned the whole thing over in her brain, again and again like a worry stone, when she looked at the whole thing this way and that, squinting with one eye closed, this time with ear to the floor looking not for "the truth" (our darling heroine felt it was all far too complex to hope for such a thing) but something which felt decent. Something she could stand. When she replayed the whole thing, which she did for the remainder of Antonio's stay on campus, two years, and a good portion of a year afterwards, what was really painful was that she recognized what Antonio felt. She could find no way to keep this knowledge from herself.

He felt—not immediately, but when her phone calls would come randomly after a year and a half, she still vaguely hinting into the silence, the abyss of his indifference, I just called to see how you are, *again*—she was sure that he felt she was ridiculous. He might have told his friends, bragged and then laughed. He felt, well, perhaps not exactly, but some percentage of what she felt when she saw the Middle Eastern proprietor, waving from the door of his establishment, beckoning in. She had told him, in a conversation they had on a day between the day Antonio was *supposed* to first call and the day he actually did, she had told the old man she was afraid to get involved with a married man, when the truth was, he revolted her.

Whenever they came upon each other, the learned doctor of literature and the restaurateur, she thought of nothing but how to get away from him because he would ask her for something and she would feel guilty refusing.

Yes, there came the day in which that quality crept into Antonio's voice. The quality of escape.

Oh, but let's go further back. Let's go into just a bit of detail about their three-week affair. He called on Sunday and a few days later she drove them to a small establishment by the side of the highway.

She held him by the chin and told him that she would have to trust him two hundred percent. Her reputation was on the line. He assured her. She said she didn't appreciate his calling six days late. That was a dis' she said, and he smiled with discomfort and promised not to do it again.

She liked his hands, his lanky fingers, and she touched them continuously as they spoke. He was studying existentialism. "Love is recognition," he said, quoting the great existentialist. Yes, she said. I see me in you and I like it. That idea brought them to intimacy. They leaned in to kiss, but then he said this, and it made her mad: he said there is a basic understanding and the rest is a game.

Then he said he was objective. This is when she smiled condescendingly at the dear sweet boy. No one is objective, she said softly. You have to be objective to play chess, he said, how can you play chess without being objective? She felt the argument was silly and she didn't even bother. She smiled as if she would reach out and pat him on the head.

When she looked back, she would think of this as the moment in which he began to store up anger, when she told him he was not objective and nearly laughed. She remembered his face in that moment. The expression of withdrawal, recalculating.

Small talk: where she was from. The social structure of that town. His intense love for his grandmother. He had dated a Russian girl for some time. Maya felt a hot rush and asked if the girl were in her class. No, he said—his turn to laugh—this was back home in the city where he was raised. She was still a bit jealous as they had shared a space behind the iron curtain. She talked about X and Y; this seemed to bore him. She talked about Alstov's discussion of ritual. He liked this topic better.

Maya had purposely not shaved her legs, which had been cultivating for some time, so she wouldn't be tempted to consummate on the first date. She didn't want to feel too sexy. Then she invited him over anyway, thinking she'd have him wait while she showered. He declined. She was embarrassed.

For the second date, he simply came over and they made love sweetly, with their eyes slit open and the lights on. Then they had sex constantly for a week and a half.

Then came a day in which Antonio was distracted. He came over late, and he kept his hands in his pockets, looking off, jingling keys, coins.

Though she tried not to take it personally, though she made no conscious decision to retaliate, there was an equal and opposite reaction.

He had touched her strangely that day. He kissed her by licking and pulled her hair. She hated the way he was kissing her and turned away. It brought up memories of the old man fucking her, and having been hurt by his distraction, she enjoyed the power of not desiring him for that one split second.

She did not set out to do it. She did not say to herself, now I will reject him because he is not looking at me dreamily and won't tell me his problems. But when the opportunity arose, yes, she felt weak and wanted to compensate.

"You don't like it?" he asked suddenly, with his eyes wide and nervous, in the same obsequious way he had said, "When should I call?" She stepped back, pulled away, went to grab another beer from the fridge; he darted forward suddenly with that embarrassing awkwardness that sometimes arose in her, as if a car had honked. As if he had distractedly walked into the middle of traffic and had to jump to safety.

She returned with the beers, feeling bad. No no no, I do like it, she said, though it had indeed repulsed her, the licking of her face, and she had indeed enjoyed, or felt the need for, the power of reject-ing him. And so she kissed him, and this time he pulled away. He had made the swing from that crumbling insecurity to anger and he never went back. That would be another moment Maya would take with her forever, in recalling the affair. First she stepping back, and then he stepping back with his final expression of recalculating. He would never show her his nerves again.

And they had sex. And then he sat on the edge of the bed smok-ing and talked and he said he had been with older women before and she said she had a lover who was a wealthy Middle Eastern businessman. That it was recent. Etc., etc. The next time they were together he refused to kiss her altogether. He said he was sexed out, and it was forever that he was stepping back, set jaw recalculating, and she, eyes widening, was the one to say, "You don't like it?"

We'll conclude with the day she was teaching. The class had deteriorated into what C and Y, back in the days of their conspiracy and complicit understanding, had not-so-affectionately dubbed the "Ricki Lake discussion." This is when the students start yelling at each other about some controversial topic not necessarily related to the text. It was what C and Y found themselves doing when what they had prepared fell well short. Maya had done this, well, again, not set out consciously to do this, but allowed it to happen, because she was depressed, didn't want to be depended on for anything, wanted the class to run without her.

Self-determination vs. fatalism, bla bla bla.

Someone said that all things happen for a reason.

Maya got on her soapbox. She noticed her own saliva in the air.

How can you say that, she bellowed, when some people are simply born, suffer and die?

Marguerite, with her effervescent glow, her glorious youthful pimple, she said, "If you believe in the theory of recognition . . ."

"The theory of recognition?"

"I mean," Marguerite blushed, "reincarnation." In that same moment, Maya noticed the Heir Apparent looking at her with that half-cocked smile. Strike that—no, it was maniacal, demonic.

She recalled the voice of Antonio's roommate.

The initiation of the panic she would not remember. There were a few moments missing from her memory, but she would remember the realization that the only thing she could possibly stand to do was to flee that room instantly. Excuse me, she said, and shoved her things in her briefcase and ran. She remembered sensing, not even seeing, but sensing, the students turning to each other with question.

She had to have someone something. Someone something had to tell her what was to come. She felt she had been loved mockingly. She felt she had been loved like we prod with a stick, from a distance. She had been loved like we turn from a gruesome moment, like something we can hardly tolerate. She just wanted to know when it would be better.

She drove to the city: She left the class. Went home. Used the restroom, stopped at the bank machine and drove the hours to the city with the radio up very loud, singing along. She remembered a gypsy card reader she had once seen in a shop window.

The gypsy didn't come in until evening, so she had hours to kill. She expected recognition. She expected something, not everything, but something that the reader would see in the tarot cards would be true, would be something she could believe in. And if not, it would be heads when she wanted tails and then she could embrace tails. She went to the park, rode the subway to get there. She sank heavily back in her seat, loving the anonymity of the city. There was comfort. There, yes, she said to herself, is comfort.

Maya walked through the park measuring her moments of peace like contractions in reverse—yes, there, three minutes, thank you. On the ride back, a girl threw M&M's at her. A girl of fourteen on the subway with nothing better to do, showing off for her peers, a group of girls picking enemies, and one of them was pelting M&M's and Maya was the target. The good doctor said to herself, yes, I could bop that child one good. I could shoot her a look of the damned and make her know it.

An M&M landed gently in Maya's lap. Another flicked her neck. She got out to switch cars, but didn't move quickly enough and had to wait for the next train.

It was beginning to grow dark when she arrived at the establishment of Veronica the gypsy. It was a little room upstairs, one flight over traffic, a little alcove with huge windows so anyone from the street could see. Maya braced herself and climbed the stairs. There was no one in the front room but she heard voices from behind a curtain. "Hello," she called and someone answered, just a minute.

The good doctor made herself comfortable in a metal folding chair, and eventually Veronica the gypsy, shuffling the tarot as she walked, joined her.

The first thing Veronica did was scour traffic. She seemed to be checking every car, waiting for, watching for, someone. She was a younger woman than Maya had hoped, her own age perhaps. How could wisdom come in the form of her contemporary? Veronica was a very pale woman, with dark kinky hair tied back into a bun at the base of her neck. She had freckles and almond eyes. She had several teeth missing, a very deep raspy voice and a heavy Brooklyn accent. She was watching cars. This one? No, not that. This? No.

They began the reading and Veronica shuffled and had Maya cut the deck. Veronica watched cars over her shoulder as she spoke. Veronica scoured traffic. Bla bla bla you have a blockage. You bla bla bla in July. Maya couldn't follow what was being said, so profoundly affronted was she by the clairvoyant's distraction. There is a man who went away, said Veronica, and when I lay down this card, you say his name, but Maya was too aware of the omnipresent jury and was sure they would know the age of her lover and was resolutely ashamed and could not say it and only shrugged. Veronica went back to the traffic, and Maya was angry that the gypsy did not try harder to make her say it. Then the woman said do you have any questions, and Maya said, yes, when will I be happy?

July, said the gypsy, squinting out the window. And when it was all over Dr. Capistrano paid her twenty-five dollars. Veronica said for a mere fifteen more she would burn special candles and our darling heroine declined.

Lara Stapleton was born and raised, primarily in East Lansing, Michigan, and for some time in Manila, Philippines. She received her B.A. from the University of Michigan and her M.A. from New York University. She lives in New York City, where she teaches for the Pratt Institute and for Long Island University in Brooklyn, and is currently working on her first novel. Her short stories have appeared in *The Antioch Review, The Glimmer Train, The Alaska Quarterly Review, Michigan Quarterly Review, Indiana Review, Chatahoochee Review, The Asian-American Pacific Journal, The New Orleans Review*, among others. She is the recipient of a 1996 Ludwig Vogelstein Foundation Grant for writers and a two-time winner of the University of Michigan's Hopwood award for fiction. She is also the winner of the 1998 *Columbia Journal* fiction prize. *The Lowest Blue Flame Before Nothing* is her first collection of short stories.

aunt lute books is a multicultural women's press that has been committed to publishing high quality, culturally diverse literature since 1982. In 1990, the Aunt Lute Foundation was formed as a non-profit corporation to publish and distribute books that reflect the complex truths of women's lives and the possibilities for personal and social change. We seek work that explores the specificities of the very different histories from which we come, and that examines the intersections between the borders we all inhabit.

Please write, phone or e-mail (books@auntlute.com) us if you would like us to send you a free catalog of our other books or if you wish to be on our mailing list for future titles. You may buy books directly from us by phoning in a credit card order or mailing a check with the catalog order form.

Please visit our website at www.auntlute.com.

Aunt Lute Books
P.O.Box 410687
San Francisco, CA 94141
(415)826-1300

This book would not have been possible without the kind contributions of the Aunt Lute Founding Friends:

Anonymous Donor
Anonymous Donor
Rusty Barcelo
Marian Bremer
Diane Goldstein

Diana Harris
Phoebe Robins Hunter
Diane Mosbacher, M.D., Ph.D.
William Preston, Jr.
Elise Rymer Turner